DATE		
OCT 19 1993		OCT 01 97
NOV 10 1993	APR 6 1995	
NOV 15 1993	OCT 02 1995	MAY 22 1998
JAN 03 1993	OCT 27 1995	OCT 03 2003
JAN 20 1994	FEB 26 1996	FEB 18 2005
NOV 07 1994		OCT 19 2005
DEC 08 1994	FEB 28 1997	APR 19 2006
	MAY 30 97	MAY 07 2012
APR 1995	NOV 19 97	

OCT 23 1995   APR 23 1998
MAR 18 1996   JUN 15 1998
JUN 12 1996

JAN 29 1997   JUN 07 2002

JAN 30 2009   MAY 31 2005

        DEC 06 2010   MAY 24 2006
OCT 09 2014   APR 16 2012

LOVING
Someone Else

ELLEN
CONFORD

LOVING

Someone Else

BANTAM BOOKS

New York • Toronto • London • Sydney • Auckland

LOVING SOMEONE ELSE
A Bantam Book / August 1991

*The Starfire logo is a registered trademark of Bantam Books,
a division of Bantam Doubleday Dell Publishing Group, Inc.
Registered in U.S. Patent and Trademark Office and elsewhere.*

Library of Congress Cataloging-in-Publication Data

Conford, Ellen.
    Loving someone else / Ellen Conford.
        p.   cm.
    Summary: To earn money for her college tuition, Holly, a
formerly rich seventeen-year-old, foregoes a summer of shopping to work for two elderly sisters on Harmony Island.
    ISBN 0-553-07353-2
    [1. Work—Fiction.   2. Old age—Fiction.]   I. Title.
PZ7.C7593Lo   1991
[Fic]—dc20
                                            90-45441
                                               CIP
                                                AC

Published simultaneously in the United States and Canada

---

*Bantam Books are published by Bantam Books, a division of
Bantam Doubleday Dell Publishing Group, Inc. Its trademark,
consisting of the words "Bantam Books" and the portrayal of a
rooster, is Registered in U.S. Patent and Trademark Office and
in other countries. Marca Registrada. Bantam Books, 666 Fifth
Avenue, New York, New York 10103.*

PRINTED IN THE UNITED STATES OF AMERICA

BVG   0 9 8 7 6 5 4 3 2

LOVING
Someone Else

1

Going to work for the Brewster sisters was not the most sensible career move I ever made, but they paid more than McDonald's and I needed the money.

If I knew then what I know now, would I have taken the job? Probably. For eight dollars an hour I would have taught chickens to tap dance.

And then there was Avery Hadden, their extremely gorgeous and extremely rich young nephew who might—if I played my cards right—marry me and support me in a life of luxury and ease till death did us part.

I was two months away from high-school graduation and was planning a summer of freedom before going to Sarah Lawrence College in September. It was a Tuesday afternoon, and my sister Sloane and I were getting ready for a few hours of serious shopping, even though she said that everyone in college wore jeans all the time, and you could always tell who the freshmen were because they were invariably overdressed.

It was at this moment, just as my life was bright with promise, that my mother sat us down and told us that she had some unpleasant news.

That was the understatement of the century.

"I'm afraid you can't go back to Yale," she told Sloane. "And you won't be able to go to Sarah Lawrence," she told me.

"Why not?" we asked.

"Our company got absorbed in a hostile takeover."

Now, I am no whiz at business, but even I can figure out that a hostile takeover is not good news.

"Your father's out," she went on, "and I have to go back to teaching and we can't afford to send you to Yale and Sarah Lawrence."

She burst into tears, which was exactly what I wanted to do, but I couldn't because I didn't want her to feel any worse than she already did.

In one horrible moment the entire course of my life was changed. All my hopes and dreams, the things I had anticipated for so long, suddenly evaporated.

"This certainly puts a damper on our shopping expedition." Sloane managed a sickly grin. My mother cried harder.

"I can't go to college?" I asked, stunned.

"We can't afford Sarah Lawrence," my mother said. "You'll have to go to Unity."

Not Unity. Anywhere but there. It was a two-year community college that accepted everyone, regardless of race, color, or species. Their entrance requirements were that you be free of communicable diseases and that you walked erect.

Unity Community. It was a joke.

"And you'll have to transfer to the state university," my mother said to Sloane. "Unless you can find someone to lend you twenty thousand dollars."

It didn't take me long to decide that if Unity was my only choice, I didn't want to go to college. I would take a job instead and pay my own way through Sarah Lawrence. It would take a lot longer, but it would be worth it.

It was in this frame of mind, the day after graduation, that I responded to the ad in the help-wanted column of the newspaper.

"Perfect for student. Companion wanted. Two adult women, charming landmark house in picturesque summer colony. Very light duties, plenty of free time, $8.00 an hour."

The ad was three days old. "I hope no one's got the job yet," I said to Sloane. "It sounds perfect."

"Too perfect," she said. "There has to be a catch somewhere."

But when I called they told me to come for an interview the next day, and that eight dollars an hour was not a misprint.

How bad could it be? They were adults, not children. You never had to chase adults around the house to get them to go to bed. And they never mixed drain cleaner with turpentine and orange juice and tried to trick you into drinking it.

I figured they were old and frail and just needed someone to dust a bit and to call the doctor in case of an emergency.

The next day I borrowed Sloane's car, which was going to be sold, and drove out to Windsor Point, where I could get the ferry to Harmony Island.

There were no bridges to the island, and unless you were a fish, the ferry was the only way to get there. The trip took forty-five minutes and was hardly a pleasure cruise. I sat in the car on the lower deck, sandwiched between other cars, so that I wasn't able to see anything remotely picturesque on the way.

I opened the car window hoping to feel the tang of fresh salt spray on my cheek, but all I smelled was gasoline, so I closed the window.

When the ferry docked I followed the car in front of me down a ramp and onto a graveled area, which led to the road.

One of the Ms. Brewsters had given me directions from the ferry slip. There was only time for a quick look around, because someone in a car behind me was leaning on a horn impatiently.

"All right, all right!" I yelled. I had the windows closed and the air conditioner on, so the driver couldn't hear me, but the outburst relieved some of my tension.

Near the pier was a dilapidated wooden building with a sign that read PRIOR'S BOATING AND FISHING: BAIT, BEER, BLOODWORMS, BOATS.

Vampire worms, I thought. What a great place to film a horror movie. "Picturesque small-town beach community terrorized by man-eating fish bait."

But I couldn't stop to cast the movie, because the

driver behind me was still going berserk with his horn. I turned around and saw that it wasn't a he, but a she, and she was driving a green Jaguar.

I couldn't hear what she yelled at me, but I had no trouble interpreting her crude hand gesture.

What a warm welcome to Harmony Island. I wondered if all the natives were this harmonious.

I followed a sign that pointed to Harmony Hill Road and turned right. Past the pier and the parking lot the road became so narrow that I was sure two cars couldn't pass each other without scraping sides, and there was hardly any shoulder. I stayed as close to the right as I could, but the road was barely broad enough for half a car.

Just as I crept past a NO PASSING sign, I heard a honk that sounded familiar.

Still leaning on the horn, the girl in the green Jaguar shot out from behind me, right into the oncoming lane. She zoomed past me, as if she didn't care if either of us emerged from this encounter alive.

"Idiot!" I screamed. "Moron!" She couldn't hear me, but it had to be said. I stopped the car for a moment to recover. I opened my window and took a few deep breaths to calm myself. The air smelled fresh and piney and green. I continued up Harmony Hill Road and found that it was actually possible for cars to pass me without colliding.

The road widened a little as I came to a stop sign. I turned right, and moments later I saw the house. It was the loneliest-looking house I had ever seen. It was large and gray, with a widow's walk and turrets that made me think of *The House of the Seven Gables*.

Definitely a good setting for a horror movie. No wonder the job was still open. I was ready to turn around and go home, and maybe even work at McDonald's.

But eight dollars an hour!

There was no driveway, only a rutty dirt path that led to a ramshackle garage with peeling gray paint that matched the house.

I parked in front of the garage. Eight dollars an hour, I reminded myself. Sixty-four dollars a day.

I got out of the car and walked toward the house. The door opened as I approached, and a small woman wearing a red plaid kilt and red sneakers waved at me. I waved back, and she waved again. Figuring this could go on all morning, I stopped waving and hustled the rest of the way to the house.

"You must be Holly Campion," she said. Her voice was high and chirpy. "Campion the Companion. Quite a coincidence, don't you think?"

I hadn't made the connection myself, and when she did, I thought of Unity Community and was nearly ready to bolt.

"I am Birdie Brewster," she said. I had to dig my nails into my palms to keep from giggling. She sounded like a bird, and I had never seen an old woman wearing such a short skirt. She was hardly my idea of a little old lady, but she didn't look dangerous, so I followed her inside.

The house was dank and musty, and I shivered as she led me into the living room. Sitting on a green plush sofa was a large, tanned woman in a pink sweat suit. She had a cane at her feet. I didn't have time to wonder why a person who needed a cane wore a sweat

wasn't likely to be Blossom, with her bad hip and the cane.

I followed Birdie upstairs. She parted the strands of floor-length red beads that hung in a doorway like a curtain.

"This is my room," she said proudly. "I used to be in show business," she added.

I didn't doubt it for a minute. Photo albums and scrap books were scattered all over the room, piled on chairs, stacked on the mantelpiece.

"Blossom keeps nagging at me to put them in the attic," Birdie said. "But I need them handy for my memoirs."

I wondered what kind of memoir she was writing. Maybe she'd been famous once.

As if she'd read my mind, Birdie said, "Oh, I was never a really *big* star, but I've had a very interesting life. I thought maybe you could help me—"

I heard a male voice from downstairs and the sound of a door closing.

"That's Avery!" Birdie's whole face lit up. "My nephew. You'll just love him."

She nearly bounced downstairs.

Standing in the center of the hallway, halfway between the stairs and the front door, was a tall man with intense blue eyes and almost black hair. He was wearing jeans and a fisherman's sweater. He looked extremely gorgeous in his jeans and fisherman's sweater, but he would have looked extremely gorgeous in a horse blanket.

"Avery!" Birdie threw her arms around his waist. "We've missed you."

9

"But I come every weekend," he said, hugging her.

"Well, we miss you during the week."

I just stood there, frozen on the staircase, gazing at him, unable to say a word. My heart was the only part of me that moved, and he could probably hear it pounding.

"Hello," he said pleasantly. "Are you going to take care of my aunts?"

He came to see them *every weekend.*

"Yes," I said.

Birdie was right. I just loved him.

"I don't think the job will be too demanding," Avery said. "It's just that with Blossom's hip and Birdie's arthritis, I thought it would be a good idea to have someone in the house with them."

I nodded. "Good idea," I repeated. "Someone in the house." I wasn't thinking too clearly. I was blinded by Avery's shining gorgeousness.

"In case of an emergency," he said.

"Emergency." I nodded.

"This house is kind of old, and Harmony Island is not a very exciting place. But the beach is great, and during the season it's pretty lively."

"Lively," I agreed.

He gave me a puzzled look. If I maintained this level of conversation he would think my IQ was too low to take care of his gerbils, let alone his aunts.

I tried to get a grip on myself. I knew there were questions I ought to be asking, but I couldn't think of them. For the moment, all that mattered was that this incredible Greek god of a person came here every weekend.

"And where are her references?" Blossom demanded. "We don't know a thing about her."

"She doesn't know a thing about us either," Birdie said.

"Do you have any references?" Avery asked. "Where did you last work?"

"I never worked," I said. "I went to school. I just graduated."

"So this will be your first job?" Blossom asked. "What about your family? Where do you live?"

"I live in Cedar Grove." Or I used to. By this time the house might be sold. "My family is—" Poor but honest? No, anything but that. "You could call my school," I suggested. At least the guidance counselor could tell the Brewsters that I was a good student and wasn't a serial killer.

"Good idea," said Avery. I breathed a sigh of relief and scribbled out St. Evangeline's address and phone number.

"And I guess you could call my mother." Just don't expect her to say very much.

"I still think this is absolutely unnecessary," Blossom grumbled. "And a waste of money. Eight dollars an hour for a baby-sitter."

"But I'm paying, Blossom," he said. "And I'm glad to do it."

"A waste of good money," she insisted.

"He can afford it," Birdie said. "And no one would take the job when we offered less."

Avery would pay my salary. Eight dollars an hour. Sixty-four dollars a day. Three hundred and twenty dollars a week. Thirteen hundred dollars a month.

Finally something besides Avery's physical magnetism penetrated my brain. He wasn't merely handsome. He was *rich*. He had to be. Who else could afford to pay me thirteen hundred dollars a month?

Rich *and* gorgeous.

This, I realized instantly, was destiny. I'd been fated to meet Avery Hadden. That's why I was led to this isolated island, this weird old house, and his weird old aunts.

I pictured myself throwing open the windows in the gloomy parlor and letting in fresh air and sunshine. I pictured Blossom and Birdie flourishing and cheerful with a dynamic young person like me influencing them.

I pictured Avery, at first feeling merely gratitude toward me for taking such terrific care of his aunts. Then, gradually—let's say by the end of August—discovering that gratitude was not all he felt for me.

If we didn't have a fancy wedding, I could be married by Labor Day. And there would still be time to start Sarah Lawrence in September.

This is ridiculous, I told myself. I'm making up a juvenile, teenage fantasy. The man is probably thirty years old and married for all I know. This is not a rational way to choose a job.

I eyed the fourth finger of his left hand. No wedding ring.

"I can start tomorrow," I said.

2

What am I doing here?

I looked around my room and had to close my eyes. Blossom may have been a good housekeeper, but she had absolutely no aptitude for interior decorating.

The walls were painted yellow, and the flowered bedspread was green and pink. The furniture was blond and had probably been modern forty years ago. It didn't go well with the yellow walls. The ruffled curtains were also yellow, but not the same shade as the walls or the furniture.

The carpet was orange. On the table next to my bed was another green ceramic horse lamp. Blossom must have gotten a discount on horse lamps.

Why hadn't I checked out my living quarters before taking this job?

Because, I reminded myself, after meeting Avery I

didn't care what the living quarters looked like. The fringe benefit was enormous.

Besides, no matter how ugly and old this house was, at least it was no place like home.

The big, cheerful house I'd grown up in didn't exist anymore. It was still there, but it would soon be sold. Maybe it was just as well. I could feel the gloom seeping from the walls.

My father had always given me unconditional love and a limitless supply of money. Now he seemed to have shrunk into himself so deeply that he was nearly invisible.

Meals were the worst. My mother said little, and my father stared down at his food, which he didn't eat. Sloane and I tried to finish as quickly as possible so we could escape to our own rooms.

These days, not being at home was a relief.

But here? In this room? In this house?

Maybe it would look more cheerful after I added a few personal touches. But what I had brought was mostly clothes and shoes and underwear. I hadn't known how badly my room would need personal touches.

I put my Walkman on the night table and my Watchman on the dresser. They didn't do much to improve the decor.

As I was stowing my underwear into a dresser drawer, I heard a soft thunk. I looked up. There was a young man trying to climb in the window. He had a hammer in his hand.

I screamed.

I heard one of the sisters calling me, but I couldn't make out what she said.

"I'm a companion." I used to have maids myself, I wanted to say. But the truth was, the difference between a maid and a companion was not great. Especially since I had to do the laundry.

"Your ice cream's ready." Duffy put two cardboard containers on the counter.

"I'll see you later," Pete said to me. "I have to stop at the boatyard for some tools."

Chandra's eyes narrowed as she looked from Pete to me.

"The one at the ferry?" I asked.

"It's my father's. Hey, do you sail?" Pete asked.

"Only as a passenger. But I love it."

Chandra looked as if she were about to explode.

"Great," Pete said. "First day off you get we'll do it. Chandra can crew and you can dangle your fingers in the water."

Chandra shot daggers at me with her eyes. It would not be safe to be on a sailboat with her. My fingers wouldn't be all that dangled from the boat.

I'm no woman of the world, but I'd had some romantic experiences, and I'd watched my friends flirting and dating and having crushes.

It seemed perfectly obvious to me. Didn't Pete realize how she felt about him?

"That sounds wonderful," I said. I had no amorous feelings toward Pete. I was saving myself for Avery. But I *did* love sailing, and I enjoyed seeing the deep shade of red Chandra's face was turning.

"I really have to go," I said. "The Brewsters are waiting for me."

"I'll be back to the house later," Pete said. "I've got

some more work to do on that shutter. In fact, I may have to stay a while and fix several shutters."

If Chandra turned any redder she'd go up in flames.

"Nice meeting you, Chandra," I lied.

For a moment I almost didn't mind being a maid.

3

"Did you say this car had power steering?" I asked Blossom.

"Yes. It's a pleasure to drive, don't you think?"

No, I don't think. The steering wheel was stiff, the hearse felt big and clumsy, and it was half a car too large for Harmony Hill Road.

I drove back to the house at a snail's pace.

"I don't mean to rush you, dear," Birdie said, "but *Divorce Court* is going to be on in five minutes."

The judge was just rapping his gavel when Birdie turned on the television in the living room. She settled down on the couch.

Blossom handed me the package of ice cream. "Put this away. And you can make us *lunco* now." She sat down next to her sister and folded her hands in her lap, as if she planned to stay there.

"Lunch, right?" I asked. "What do you want me to make?"

"Make some sandwiches," Blossom said.

That I could do. "What kind?"

"For heaven's sake, Holly," she said irritably, "use your head. Now that you're here I'm not supposed to have to think about things like that."

She dismissed me with a wave of her hand and turned back to the TV.

In the kitchen I checked the drawers and cabinets to see what was where. They had a lot of canned soups. I was good at canned soups, so I pulled out a can of tomato.

I figured since there were just the two of them in the house, and they had bought the food themselves, they'd like whatever I prepared.

I took a large can of salmon from a cabinet and looked around for a can opener. I couldn't find one. It wasn't on the counter, it wasn't next to the stove. I turned 360 degrees around the kitchen without seeing it.

I went back to the living room. "I can't find the can opener," I said.

"It's in the drawer next to the sink," Blossom answered.

"It fits in a drawer?" That was a surprise.

"It's a can opener," Blossom said impatiently. "Of course it fits in a drawer."

"Oh, right," I said, finally understanding. "I just assumed you had an electric one."

"Shh," said Birdie, leaning toward the TV.

"Why would you assume that?" Blossom asked.

24

"I—uh—" I thought everyone had an electric can opener.

Back in the kitchen I made three salmon sandwiches and heated up the soup. I'd never seen a stove like theirs. It was yellow and tall and had two ovens and oversized on-off knobs for the range. It was certainly old, but it worked just fine.

I opened all the base cabinets in the kitchen looking for trays. I was sure they wouldn't want to miss any of *Divorce Court*. I found a large tray, with a colorful picture of palm trees and hula dancers painted on it. When everything was ready I laid out two plates and two soup bowls and spoons and brought everything into the living room.

"Good," said Blossom. "Just put it on the coffee table." She reached for a bowl of soup. "Where's your lunch? Aren't you hungry?"

"I was going to eat in the kitchen," I said. That's where our maid always ate.

"Don't be silly," Blossom said. "You'll eat with us."

"*Shh!*" Birdie reached for her sandwich without taking her eyes from the TV screen. "Here comes the mother-in-law."

"Well, okay," I said. "I'll bring my lunch in. Thank you."

"What are you thanking me for?" Blossom asked.

"SHHHH!"

When *Divorce Court* was over it was time to clean up the lunch dishes. I couldn't find a dishwasher, and since that couldn't possibly fit into a drawer, I resigned myself to manual dishwashing.

I decided to make very simple meals from then on, to keep cleanup to a minimum. I didn't know how to cook anyway, so it was an easy decision to make.

After I finished the dishes Blossom handed me a feather duster and told me to dust. Everything.

I examined the furniture in the living room. "But it's not dusty."

"The time to dust is before you see the dust collecting," she said.

"Blossom is a meticulous housekeeper," Birdie said.

I didn't doubt it for a minute.

"Be especially careful of that." Blossom pointed to a pale green Chinese vase on the mantelpiece.

"Is it valuable?" I wondered if there was a Ming dynasty piece somewhere in this jumble of assorted junk.

"The urn itself is not particularly valuable, but that's where I keep Mr. Brewster's ashes."

"Ashes?" I stared at the urn. "Mr. Brewster's ashes?"

"My husband," Blossom said. "This was the finest urn that his funeral home offered. So when he was cremated I put his ashes in there. This way he is always near me."

I wondered what a person's ashes looked like. Did they fill the whole urn, or were the remains no more than a handful of dust?

"And they give me something to focus on when I speak to him."

"You speak to him? You speak to the ashes?" Uh oh.

"No," she said. "I speak to Mr. Brewster. But we hold the seance in here to be close to his physical essence."

"Seance," I repeated stupidly.

"I'm sure he'll want to meet you," she said. "He's still so devoted to me."

I had a feeling that the other applicants for this job had met Mr. Brewster before I did. No wonder the Brewsters had had trouble getting help.

I wondered if Avery was a spiritualist too. I didn't think it very likely. It was probably Avery who told Blossom not to mention Mr. Brewster until after I took the job.

"When you finish dusting," Blossom said, "you can start studying your Esperanto."

Eight dollars an hour suddenly seemed like a lot less money than it had two days ago.

That night I lay on my *lito*, unable to get to *dormo*. I thought about the people I had met that day. Chandra was a snob and a snot, and Mr. Brewster was dead.

Blossom was, at the very least, eccentric, if not delusional. She assured me that when she spoke to Mr. Brewster at their weekly seances, he always spoke back. She didn't say what he talked about. Maybe he told her how often to lube the hearse.

Birdie was sweet, and Pete, thank goodness, seemed normal. If it weren't for them, I realized, I would never stay on here. Eight dollars an hour or not.

Avery Hadden or not.

The longer I lay there not sleeping, the more homesick I became. I couldn't understand why. I'd spent five years at summer camp. I'd taken teen tours of Canada and Switzerland, and I'd been fine.

And now that home was a place I didn't want to be, it seemed strange that I should miss it.

I imagined what they were doing right this minute. My father was probably sitting in the den with a book on his lap, not reading it. My mother was probably in front of the TV, not watching it.

Even thinking about them hurt. But I was so alone. I thought about phoning my sister collect, but I'd upset her and my mother if I told them how bad I felt.

And soon I understood that what I missed was not my house, but my home the way it used to be, my family the way we used to be.

Would it ever get better? Would we ever get better?

I couldn't go back to the home of my childhood, no matter how hard I wished it.

I might as well stay here. Supporting myself was the only way I could help them. If I were going to be miserable anyway, I might as well be miserable for sixty-four dollars a day.

4

The only thing worse than trying to fall asleep in my room was waking up in it. It was so *yellow*. And orange. And green. I needed sunglasses. Or better yet, a blindfold.

I squinted at the electric clock next to my bed. Seven-fifteen. I groaned and squashed my face into the pillow. The last time I'd looked at the clock it was two o'clock, and I was still listening to my Walkman.

But I heard bathroom noises. And footsteps on the stairs. The Brewsters were awake and going to stay awake. Sure. They hadn't had only five hours of sleep.

I dragged myself out of bed. They'd expect breakfast. I could handle toast and eggs, but I'd have to confess that I couldn't make coffee. I didn't drink it myself, so I never bothered to learn how.

I pulled on shorts and a T-shirt, slipped into my sandals, and staggered downstairs. I needed toothpicks to hold my eyelids open.

The sisters looked surprised when I limped into the kitchen.

"You didn't have to get up this early, dear," Birdie said. She was wearing a black silk kimono with a huge embroidered red-and-green dragon on the front. "We know that teenagers like to sleep late."

Blossom nodded. "Old people get up early."

"You're only as old as you feel," Birdie said.

"I feel old," Blossom grumbled.

"But I'm supposed to cook," I said. "Can I make you some eggs?"

"No!" Birdie's voice cracked.

"Are you watching your cholesterol?" I asked.

"She doesn't eat anything yellow," Blossom said.

"I had a terrible experience with an ear of corn a few years ago," Birdie said.

What kind of terrible experience could you have with an ear of corn?

Blossom pointed to her teeth. "Dentures," she said in a stage whisper. "Got stuck."

"Well, how about some bacon then?" I'd never cooked bacon, but how hard could it be?

"I don't eat meat," Blossom said.

"You're a vegetarian?"

"No. I eat fish, but I don't eat meat. It overtaxes the digestive system."

"Cold cereal?" Pouring milk over cornflakes was one of my few culinary skills. "You don't eat Rice Krispies or anything like that, do you?" What was there left to eat for breakfast?

"Oatmeal," Birdie said. "We like oatmeal."

"Okay, I'll make oatmeal. It's the kind where you just add boiling water, right?"

"No," said Blossom. "It's the kind you have to cook and stir for fifteen minutes."

What kind of cereal had to be cooked for fifteen minutes? I'd never eaten one that took more than ninety seconds to prepare.

I scanned the kitchen. "You know," I said, "you could have your oatmeal in two minutes if you used a microwave."

"We're not usually in much of a hurry," Birdie said.

"Besides," added Blossom, "they transmit dangerous vibrations."

I sighed. "Where's the oatmeal?"

Obviously it was going to be another day of new experiences for me. I'd never stood at a stove for more than three minutes in my entire life.

Even though the back door was open to let in a light morning breeze, it was steamy standing over the bubbling oatmeal.

"Ms. Brewster," I said, "doesn't it bother you to be in the kitchen with a yellow stove?"

"Call me Birdie, dear. I sit with my back to it."

She must walk past my room with her eyes shut.

"The *forno* is *flava*," Blossom said.

"The furnace is flavorful?" I guessed.

"The stove is yellow. You may call *me Mrs.* Brewster."

I would call her Mrs. Brewster, but she would always be Blossom to me. I mean, how could I break up a set? Already Blossom and Birdie sounded as natural to me as salt and pepper.

"We usually do the *talajo* on Mondays," Blossom said. "But I didn't want to overtax you in your first week."

"Telephoning?" I asked.

"Laundry."

A horrible thought crossed my mind. They didn't have an electric can opener. They didn't have an automatic dishwasher. Was it possible that they didn't have—

"Do you have a washing machine?"

"Of course," said Blossom. "It's in the basement. I've been taking care of the *talajo* myself, but it's hard to get up and down the stairs. And my sister can't hang it up because of her arthritis."

"Hang it up?" I didn't think I could face any more nasty shocks in the modern-appliance department.

"Are you sure you know how to do laundry?" Blossom eyed me suspiciously.

"Yes, but the thing is, we always used a drier."

Blossom shook her head. "Electric can openers . . . automatic dishwashers . . . microwave ovens. No wonder American children are so flabby."

The basement was dank and smelled moldy. It wasn't easy carrying the loads of clothes down the narrow staircase. It was even harder carrying the wet wash back upstairs and outside. I couldn't imagine how Blossom had managed it with her injured hip.

The way I dealt with the laundry was basically not to look at anybody's underwear when I threw it into the machine. I was thankful that they didn't have one of those old wringer type washers, where you had to feed the clothes through the rollers.

For someone who claimed she didn't need me, Blossom found a lot for me to do. I went downstairs three times with three loads of wash: one white, one colored, and one of sheets and pillowcases.

In the backyard I decided that whoever had invented the electric clothesdrier deserved sainthood. I struggled to drape wet sheets over the line while a stiff wind whipped them back in my face. Blossom was several inches taller than I was, so I could barely reach the line to attach the clothespins.

Another horrible thought occurred to me as I hung up the colored wash. Would Blossom expect me to do the *ironing*?

I draw the line at ironing, I swore to myself. I am *not* a maid, I'm a companion. Companions don't iron.

I was hanging up a Hawaiian shirt—I couldn't imagine whose—when I felt a tug on the line.

"Peekaboo." Pete grinned at me over the clothesline. "Need some help with that?"

"Where were you two hours ago?"

"Working," he said. "At the boatyard."

"Want to trade jobs? I don't care *what* I have to do as long as it isn't laundry. They don't even have a *drier*."

He nodded. "They're kind of old-fashioned. But they grow on you. Listen, I think I should show you how to start the car in case you have trouble. Sometimes the butterfly valve—"

"I have to finish the wash first." I jammed a clothespin into a pair of men's pajama bottoms. Was I doing a dead man's laundry?

"It'll only take a minute," Pete said. "I taught Blossom how to do it."

"So why do I have to know how?"

"What if the car won't start when you're in town alone?" he said. "How are you going to get back to the house?"

"I'll call the boatyard and ask you to help."

He looked at me as if he were trying to figure out whether or not I was joking. "Promise?"

"Promise," I said.

"In that case, I'll never teach you how to fix the valve."

I knew that there was an element of light flirtation going on, but what harm could it do? Of course it was Avery I really wanted to flirt with, but this banter with Pete was good practice. I was between boyfriends when my father got laid off. It had been two months since I'd had a date.

"I came to ask you if you could go sailing on Sunday," he said.

"Sure, I'd love to." If Avery didn't come this weekend. "Will Chandra be there?"

"Not if you don't want her to be. But she's a good sailor. It helps to have another sailor along."

"Oh, let her come," I said. I could be generous. Besides, it would do my ego good to watch her seethe as Pete flirted with me. "I don't mind her that much."

I felt tolerant and triumphant. I had just hung up the last piece of three washloads of laundry.

"Maybe it would be better if we went alone," he said thoughtfully.

I picked up the empty laundry bag and batted my eyelashes at him.

"Maybe it would."

5

"Time for *lunco*," Blossom announced as I walked in the kitchen door.

My good mood evaporated. "But I just finished the *talajo*." Give me a break, I wanted to say.

"It's all ready," she said. "Melted cheese sandwiches."

My good mood returned. Blossom had prepared lunch instead of waiting for me to do it. Given a choice, I'd prefer to make three sandwiches than to wash three loads of laundry, but companions can't be choosers.

"Isn't cheese yellow?" I asked.

"Birdie eats white American cheese and Swiss cheese."

"I guess that makes it easier." No meat for Blossom, nothing yellow for Birdie. It was going to be a real challenge to plan meals for them.

We watched *Divorce Court* while we ate lunch. It

was a pretty sordid case. I peeked at Blossom and Birdie, wondering if all the sex talk embarrassed them.

Blossom shook her head a lot as if she disapproved of the whole affair, but she didn't take her eyes from the screen, not even to look at her food. Birdie watched avidly as the husband confessed to several x-rated episodes. I wasn't sure *I* approved of this show.

After *Divorce Court* was over, Birdie clapped her hands and looked at me expectantly. "Now," she said, "you can help me with my memoirs."

"Give her a chance to rest," Blossom said, to my surprise. "She just spent the whole *mateno* doing the *talajo.*"

Birdie's face fell. "I know you make fun of my memoirs, Blossom, but they mean a lot to me. I don't make fun of your silly Esperanto, do I?"

"I beg your pardon?" Blossom said coldly.

"Well, I'm sorry, Blossom, but my memoirs are as important to me as your Esperanto is to you." Birdie's voice started out firmly but grew softer as Blossom glared at her.

"Communication is the key to world peace," Blossom said. "If everyone in the world spoke Esperanto, there would be no more wars."

I looked from one sister to the other, as if I were watching a tennis game. I was sure Birdie would lose the argument. It was obvious who had the last word in this house.

"I don't mind helping Birdie," I said. It had to be less exhausting than schlepping laundry.

Blossom shrugged. "Suit yourself."

Birdie beamed. She stood up and gently pressed my hand with her gnarled fingers. "Come, dear. All the albums are in my room. I haven't been able to write for weeks. I have so many ideas backed up in my head."

"I can type pretty fast," I volunteered. "I can probably keep up with you."

"I don't have a typewriter," Birdie said. "I do everything by hand."

She led the way upstairs and through the red bead curtains into her room.

No typewriter. Of course no typewriter. Why in the world would they have a typewriter? I looked around the cluttered room, wondering where Birdie kept the inkwell and the quill pen.

She cleared a few albums off the spindly French provincial desk to make a very small work space.

"You can write at the secretary," she said. "This is what I've done so far." She handed me a sheaf of white onionskin paper. "I'm only up to 1942. You can read it later. Let's get started right now. I can feel the words just *pouring* out of me."

I picked up a blue-and-white ballpoint pen from the Drummond Fuel Company. I could almost feel my hand ache even before we began. I looked at Birdie's fingers. I had nothing to complain about.

"Now," she said, "this is a romantic part. It's World War Two and I've just met Archie. Archie was my husband." She shut her eyes as if she were seeing him again. She cleared her throat.

"I met my husband by a possibly mystical quirk of fate. I was not scheduled to perform for the troops on the night of April 12, 1943, but one of the other dancers was ill and I was asked to replace her. Have you got that, Holly?"

I shook my head. "I don't have anything after 'troops.' "

"I'll slow down. Through some strange coincidence, Archie Bennet, a handsome lieutenant in the RAF, was just recuperating from a leg wound."

"I thought your name was Brewster," I said. "Aren't you and Blossom both Brewsters?"

"No," Birdie said. "We're sisters, but she felt it would be more convenient if we both had the same last name." She looked wistful. "As she said, I was only married to Archie for a short time."

I thought that was terrible, but maybe there was a reason for it that I didn't know or wouldn't understand.

My hand hurt already. "Maybe if you dictated into a tape recorder," I suggested, "I could—"

Birdie looked blank. "A tape recorder?"

Get real, Campion. I was more likely to find a signed photo of Abraham Lincoln in this place.

"I'll go very, very slowly," she said. "It's just that it's so exciting to be able to write again."

". . . recuperating from a leg wound," I reminded her.

"Some of his mates were going to the USO show, and they urged Archie to go with them."

Even the pen and the paper were uncomfortably clumsy to work with. I had to press down very hard to get a visible line of print on the thin, filmy paper, but if I pressed too hard the pen went right through it.

"Archie's wound was still plaguing him, and walking

was painful. But he had never seen a USO show before, and his friends insisted that the entertainment would lift his spirits."

Her voice grew soft and dreamy. "From the moment I began to dance I could see that the dashing RAF lieutenant was watching me. He rested his hands on his cane and just gazed at me all the while I was on stage. After the show—"

I heard a phone ring. I looked around the room, but I didn't see a telephone. "Should I go and answer that?" I asked.

"Don't bother. Blossom will get it. After the show—"

"Holly!" It was Blossom's voice. "Telephone. It's Avery. He wants to speak to you."

I dropped the pen and was halfway down the stairs before she finished the sentence. I followed her voice into the kitchen. She handed me the receiver of the old black wall phone. "Probably checking up on us," she said.

"Probably checking up on *me*," I said nervously. "Hello, Mr. Hadden." I tried not to sound too breathless, but after all, I'd just raced down the stairs to speak to the man I loved.

"How's it going?" he asked. His voice sounded a little thin, but the ancient phone might have been to blame.

Blossom hovered nearby, folding a kitchen towel. But since she had to unfold it first it was pretty obvious that it didn't need folding.

"Everything's fine," I said. "I mean, it is with me."

"Is my aunt standing next to you?"

"Yes."

"Would there be anything you'd want to tell me if she wasn't?"

Nothing much. Except that I adore you, I wish you were here, and how many children should we have?

"No," I said.

"I'll be coming out Friday for the weekend," he said. "So if you'd like to get away, or go home or something—"

"Oh, no. I have no special plans." Not the kind he was thinking of.

"Okay. There's always a fireworks show on July Fourth. And the summer people will be there by then. It will be more lively for you."

It will be lively enough with you, I thought, and the fireworks I have in mind are entirely different from the ones you're thinking of.

"I'll bring your paycheck out with me," he said. "Or would it be easier if I paid you in cash?"

Pay me in cash, I thought, and dole out the bills one by one, pressing my hand every time you put a dollar in it.

"Holly?"

"Huh? Oh, fine. Good. Cash. Whatever." I cared very little about money just then. Avery was coming. He'd be here for four days. Just enough time for a whirlwind courtship.

Though he probably wouldn't propose until next week.

6

On Thursday, Blossom gave me a long list of errands to run.

"Avery's coming tomorrow, you know," she said.

If I knew? I'd been counting the hours since Tuesday.

I was delighted to run the errands, to buy his favorite foods for the special dinner I'd be making for him.

Forget that the only hot food I could prepare was canned soup. Once we were married, the cook could feed him.

I glanced down at the list. It was in Esperanto.

"Mrs. Brewster, I can't read the list."

"You can learn while you shop," she said. She turned the page over. The list was printed in English on the back. "Isn't that a good idea?"

"Good idea," I agreed. As soon as I got to town I'd ignore the Esperanto side, or it would take me forever to get things done. I hoped she didn't expect me to be fluent by the time I got back.

"Charge everything to my *kalkulo*," she said. "The shopkeepers all know me."

I didn't doubt it for a minute. Since she didn't give me any money I took a wild guess that *kalkulo* meant charge account. I was proficient in charge accounts.

I took the car keys from the hook near the back door.

"Do you remember how to get to town?" she asked.

"Sure. I'll be fine." Driving a hearse. Which I could barely steer.

When I turned the key in the ignition the engine wheezed but didn't turn over. I tried again, hitting the accelerator at exactly the same time as I turned the key. This time it sounded like someone building up to a sneeze that didn't come out.

On the third try, the engine chugged a little, but it still didn't start.

It must be the butterfly valve that Pete had talked about. I'd have to ask Blossom to start the car.

"It's very simple, really," Blossom said when I told her the problem.

The air felt like wet cotton as we walked out to the garage. Hot, humid, smelly.

"Now watch," she said. She raised the hood. "You might be stuck alone sometime."

So I'll ask Pete. He'd promised to help. Avery was coming. I couldn't get too worked up about the butterfly valve.

"This is the oil filter," she said. "You just unscrew the nut on top of it and take off the filter."

It looked like a black flying saucer.

conversation. Once I began thinking about marriage to Avery it was hard to concentrate on anything else.

"Yes," he said. "I've lived here all my life."

"What do you do in the winter? Do you go to college?"

"No. I got out of high school two years ago and I've been working at the boatyard since then."

"You're not going to college?"

"What for?" he said. "I'm going to own the boatyard. It makes a lot of money. I don't need a degree for that."

I tried to think of all the boys I'd been friends with, all the boys I'd gone out with. I couldn't remember ever knowing a boy who wasn't either in college or planning to go.

"What about you?" he asked.

"Long story," I said. "And we're almost in town."

"I can take a long lunch hour."

For weeks I'd hidden from everyone, talked to no one but Sloane, done all my crying in private. Now, all at once I felt the full force of my isolation, not only emotionally but physically on this island in the middle of the sound.

And Pete seemed strong and kind and intelligent, even if he didn't go to college. He liked me. And except for Blossom and Birdie, he was the only person here I knew.

It was cooler now as we got nearer to town. There was a light breeze, and with the truck's windows open you almost didn't need air-conditioning.

"So? Tell me your story," he said.

I shook my head. "Not now." I hadn't even told Jane

Schuster, whom I'd known since fourth grade, how devastated I was. How could I possibly tell Pete? I'd known him for three days and spent a total of fifteen minutes with him. He was a stranger.

"You're a mystery girl," he said.

"Nothing nearly that glamorous."

The traffic—if you can call seven cars traffic—increased as we drove into town. But the streets were busy now, with pale people in shorts licking ice-cream cones and peering into store windows.

I checked the English side of my list. There were a lot of groceries to be bought at the Superette, and I'd have to stop at the drugstore and someplace called Wickworld.

The only parking space big enough for Pete's truck was two blocks away from the grocery store.

"I'll go eat," he said, "and when you're finished shopping I'll bring the truck around."

We walked back toward the supermarket. Chandra's car was parked in front of the bookstore. I was glad that the Brewsters hadn't wanted any books.

"See you later," Pete said.

The Superette was half the size of any supermarket I'd ever seen, and it was crammed with shoppers. The carts created traffic jams in every aisle, and people stopping to greet each other created bigger traffic jams.

Everybody seemed to know everybody else. The summer residents must have all arrived at once, with everyone stocking up for the holiday weekend.

The only grocery shopping I'd ever done was to pick up a bottle of mineral water or a frozen pizza.

I suspected that food buying was an entirely different

skill from shopping for clothes. I hardly knew the lay-out of the supermarket we ordered from at home. It would take hours to find all the things I had to buy here, without counting waiting on the checkout line.

This promised to be as bad as doing laundry.

I pushed my cart down the first aisle I could get into. I moved slowly past the flour and sugar, and noticed a package of piecrust mix. The directions looked easy, and there was a recipe for apple pie right on the side of the box.

Apple pie, I thought. What man wouldn't love a homemade apple pie? Right above the cake mixes were cans of fruit for pies. They even had a can of apple pie filling, all prepared. No peeling, no chopping, no noth-ing. All you had to do was open the can and pour it over the piecrust.

Even without an electric can opener, what could be easier?

The rest of the shopping took almost an hour. I won-dered if Pete would still be able to drive me home. It must be past his lunch hour by now.

As I stood on the checkout line I imagined Avery's visit. Tomorrow at this time he could be eating my pie, holding my hand, planning our wedding.

Ridiculous, Campion. It would probably be weeks before he proposed.

The clerk at the counter looked at me curiously when I told her to charge the bill to Blossom.

"You with the Brewsters?" She seemed to be re-pressing a giggle.

I nodded.

"Did you meet Mr. Brewster yet?" she whispered.

"Mr. Brewster's dead," I said.

"Don't be surprised if you meet him anyway."

The woman at Wickworld didn't even ask me who I was buying candles for. I told her I needed seven white candles, which seemed like five more than we'd need to eat dinner by candlelight.

"For Mrs. Brewster," she said. "I wondered where she was this week."

"She comes in every week?"

"She certainly does." The woman picked up a handful of slim white candles from a bin. "Candles help to create the right atmosphere. The twilight between the planes of existence."

"Whatever." I shrugged.

It wasn't until I was in the drugstore that I put everything together. "Planes of existence," she'd said. And the clerk in the supermarket. "Don't be surprised if you meet Mr. Brewster."

The weekly candles were for a seance. Blossom must hold a seance every week.

Well, she could count me out. I wasn't sure what planes of existence I believed in, but I didn't want to fool around with any of them.

Unless Avery participated. And we had to hold hands around a table, in which case I'd be glad to join them, as long as I could hold Avery's hand. I'm flexible.

I came out of the drugstore with medications for both of the Brewster sisters, and saw Pete leaning against a lamp post near the Superette.

Chandra was with him. She was dressed all in white,

including a wide-brimmed white hat. She had her hand on his arm and was talking rapidly.

My shopping cart was still in front of the market, where I'd left it. Neither Pete nor Chandra noticed me as I approached them.

"But why not?" Chandra said. "It's the perfect arrangement. We can—"

"There you are," Pete said, spotting me. "Are you finished shopping?"

Chandra nearly snarled. "Pete, I want to talk to you—"

He smiled apologetically. "I've got to go," he told her. "I promised Holly I'd drive her home."

"Well, that's certainly more important than anything *I* have to say." Killer sarcasm.

"Chandra, I really don't have time for the stuff I have to do now. I can't take on anything else, not in the summer."

"But I'm only *here* for the summer. If you didn't spend so much charity time with those senile Brewsters—"

"They need me," he said. "Your father can afford to get someone else to clean your pool."

"They're not senile," I said. Crazy maybe, but not senile.

She shot me a venomous look. I regretted opening my mouth. "I can see how *overworked* you are, Pete." One more glare for each of us, and she turned on her heel and stalked away.

"I sensed a little tension in the air," I said.

"You're very observant," he replied. "She's been trying to get me to work around her place. She doesn't like to take no for an answer."

"She likes you," I said. "She wants *you*, not a pool cleaner."

"Nah. That's ancient history. She's just used to getting her way."

As we loaded the groceries into the truck, I wondered how ancient the history was.

The only easy thing about making a piecrust was opening the package of mix.

"I always make my pies from scratch," Blossom said disapprovingly.

"This is my first pie," I said. "I thought I should start with something easy."

Blossom gave me a wooden board and handed me a rolling pin. All I knew about rolling pins was that in the comics, wives hit their husbands over the head with them for coming home late.

I added water to the piecrust mix, shaped it into a ball, and put it on the board to roll it out.

"You have to use flour to keep the dough from sticking," Blossom said.

Sure enough, when I picked up the dough a good part of it stayed stuck to the board. I sprinkled flour on the board and tried to roll it out again. Half of the dough stuck to the rolling pin and then doubled over on itself.

No matter how much flour I used the dough kept sticking to something. It was hot, and I was sticky from perspiration. I wiped my forehead with a floury hand and got a small piece of dough right in my hairline.

Every attempt to roll the dough into a circle failed.

"It might be too humid to make a pie," Blossom said.

Now she tells me? Since when did you have to listen to a weather forecast before you baked something?

The pastry was starting to look dingy from all my handling. Blossom finally left me alone in the kitchen. I scraped the dough off the board with my fingernails and, cursing under my breath, hurled the pie dough across the kitchen.

It stuck to the wall.

7

Having witnessed my disaster with apple pie, Blossom would not let me into the kitchen on Friday. She was preparing a special dinner for Avery, and she said she didn't want me in the way.

That was fine with me, since the heat and humidity had grown even worse. The house, which had been so cool the first day I saw it, felt like a sauna.

My clothes were damp an hour after I dressed in the morning. I changed clothes and they just got sweaty again.

I didn't need to ask if they had an air conditioner. I spent most of the morning fantasizing about Avery and fanning myself with a copy of *Fate* magazine.

Every so often I stopped fanning myself and read an article. It was a pretty interesting magazine, all about ghosts and flying saucers and the supernatural.

Avery called at lunchtime to say he would be out

on the three-o'clock ferry. Blossom and Birdie were so excited that they didn't even watch *Divorce Court.* Instead, they set each other's hair. Blossom had thin metal curlers all over her head. She set Birdie's hair on pink plastic rollers.

"*La virino suferas cion por la beleco,*" said Blossom gaily.

"I have a pain in my stomach?" I guessed.

"Womankind suffers everything for beauty," Blossom translated.

They were upstairs removing their curlers when I decided to go to the ferry dock. It was two-thirty and the trip only took about five minutes, but I felt like I couldn't stand around and wait any longer.

I took the keys and went out to the garage.

The hearse wouldn't start.

Uh oh. Pete had been supposed to teach me how to fix it, but we'd forgotten all about it.

Blossom had half a head full of curlers when I went to tell her that I couldn't start the car.

She threw her hands up. "I thought Pete was going to show you that yesterday. Don't tell me you still can't do it."

"I'm sorry," I said. "I forgot."

If Blossom didn't limp I'm sure she would have stomped down the stairs in a rage. As it was, she muttered just loud enough for me to hear her. "I don't know what we're paying you for. You can't cook, you can't bake, you can't even run simple errands without my help. I don't know what the point is, I really don't."

"I'm *sorry,*" I repeated. Did I ask to be exiled from the kitchen? Hadn't I told them that I didn't know how to cook? And no errand was simple if it had to be run in that car.

I was about to blurt most of this out when I realized it was not a good time to start an argument with Blossom. She could have Avery send me back on the next ferry.

"Maybe you can show me how to fix it." I tried to sound humble.

"I don't have time to teach you now," she said. She raised the hood and pulled off the oil filter. She reached down and did something with the valve.

"Start the car," she ordered. I turned on the ignition. The engine turned over immediately. She jiggled something, then slammed the hood down and held out her grease-stained hands for me to see.

"A fine thing," she said. "And I just gave myself a manicure."

If I said "I'm sorry" once more I was sure I'd scream it, so I just revved the motor a few times and took off for the dock.

The car had air-conditioning, but it was 1963 air-conditioning, and not very effective. I drove slowly and joined a line of cars heading for the pier.

Even so, I still had to wait fifteen minutes for Avery's ferry.

I parked near the Boats-Bait-Beer sign. There was a cluster of people waiting for the ferry, and some activity at the boatyard, but I didn't see Pete.

Finally the ferry approached. It seemed to creep toward the dock. It took forever to slide into its berth.

I climbed out of the hearse and waved. I couldn't see

him, but a lot of other people on the ferry waved back at me.

At last I saw him striding off the boat, his jacket swung over his shoulder. He looked like a magazine advertisement for after-shave.

He smiled broadly as he walked down the ramp, as if he was really glad to see me. Almost as if he had been hoping that I would meet him and was pleasantly surprised when I did.

I was so bowled over by his obvious affection for me that I could hardly breathe.

"How's it going? Have my aunts driven you crazy yet?"

"No," I said.

He got into the passenger seat of the hearse. "I bet you were surprised, though, when you saw this car."

I got into the driver's seat. I turned the key and waited for the car to not start.

But it did. Avery fanned himself with a newspaper. "It's not much cooler here than it is in the city," he said.

I got in line behind the cars heading for Harmony Hill Road, glancing at Avery's profile every chance I got. I felt very unglamorous, hunched over the steering wheel, driving like a little old lady and perspiring from every pore.

I wished I'd asked Avery to drive so I could have looked at him all the way back to the house, but, I told myself, I could look at him all weekend.

"I brought you your first two weeks' salary," he said. "In cash."

"But I've only worked a week."

"I'm sure you wouldn't abandon my aunts and run off with the money."

"I wouldn't," I said. "But you don't know that. You don't know me at all, Mr. Hadden."

"Avery," he corrected. "And we've got the whole weekend to get acquainted, haven't we?"

I nearly drove off the side of the road, plunging us over the steep cliff to our deaths. I thought I would have to stop the car until my heart started beating normally again.

"Besides," he said, "I might not be here next week."

Not here next week? "But you said you came every weekend."

"Usually I do, but now that you're here, maybe I can take a few weekends off."

A few weekends off?

Blossom and Birdie were waiting at the door for us as I turned onto the dirt path toward the garage. Birdie was wearing a red-and-white dress with a short skirt, and Blossom was wearing a green dress with a respectable hemline. Standing side by side in the doorway they looked like Christmas.

I let Avery out and drove the car into the garage. I slammed the door behind me. Hard. I shoved the garage doors closed and jammed the padlock closed.

Avery had an aunt on each arm as he went into the house. Blossom chatted excitedly. Nobody seemed to have noticed my little temper tantrum.

I trailed behind them sulking. My terms of employment included weekly visits from Avery Hadden. I would never have taken this job if Avery wasn't a fringe benefit. Well, maybe for eight dollars an hour I might have, but that's not the point.

". . . iced *teo*," Blossom was saying. "And we're having your favorite for dinner. Nutburgers!"

When things go wrong they go wrong all the way.

Avery and his aunts settled on the sofa to sip tea and eat sugar cookies. It looked like an all-afternoon chat.

"Why don't you take some time off, Holly?" he suggested. Couldn't he wait to get rid of me? "Now that I'm here you ought to take advantage of me."

Maybe he wanted to talk about me with his aunts. But I didn't want to pass up the opportunity to spend a few hours with him. He'd said that we'd get to know each other intimately by Monday. Well, maybe he didn't say that exactly, but . . .

"I don't mind staying in," I said. "I don't have any special plans."

"Have you been to the beach yet?" he asked.

"No."

"Why not? I thought all teenagers loved going to the beach."

All teenagers? He lumped me together with all teenagers? I was outraged. Couldn't he see that I wasn't just a teenager, but a potential mate?

Blossom and Birdie frowned at me. They seemed to resent the conversation between Avery and me. I could hardly blame them. They'd waited so eagerly for his visit.

"Maybe we'll go tomorrow," he said. "We can make a whole day of it."

Did "we" mean me too?

"You're going to love Harmony Beach," he said.

Maybe this weekend would turn out all right after all.

Although I wasn't too sure of that as I ate my nutburger. Blossom had managed to find plenty for me to do, washing up behind her as she cooked, fetching things from the refrigerator, and washing and peeling vegetables.

She used a lot of vegetables. And they all needed to be peeled. Except for the sprouts. Which she also used a lot of.

The sisters grew even more animated as we ate dinner. The excitement of Avery's visit didn't subside as the hours passed.

I sat opposite Avery at the table, where I could get an eyeful of his incredible gorgeousness. But he wasn't just another pretty face, I discovered. He was witty and charming and entertaining. No wonder the aunts looked forward to his visits. When he spoke to you it was as if you were the most important person in the world, even if there were two other people there.

I felt a twinge of disappointment when Blossom served raspberries and cream for dessert. I was sorry that I couldn't present him with my home-baked apple pie. He was so lavish with praise about the nutburgers, he surely would have been impressed with a pie.

But, *c'est la vie*. Man does not live by pie alone.

"Now," Blossom said, standing, "let's get the table cleared off. Just soak the *plados*, Holly. We'll wash up later."

We all carried our plates and silverware into the kitchen, which I thought was extremely democratic. I felt a little bit less like a servant.

The aunts bustled in and out of the dining room, giddy with anticipation. I didn't know what it was they were anticipating, but I began to feel a twinge of anxiety.

When the table was completely cleared of *plados*, Blossom said, "Bring in the candles, Birdie. I'll go get Edmund."

I heard a distant rumble of thunder.

Avery laughed. "Good timing."

Blossom placed Edmund's urn in the middle of the table.

"Is this one of those seances you were talking about?" I asked.

"Yes," Birdie said. "Isn't it exciting?"

Another clap of thunder. Louder. Closer.

"Exciting is not the word I'd choose," I said.

"Have you ever been to one of these before?" Avery asked.

I shook my head. Blossom and Birdie were placing candlesticks around the dining room. Blossom put two on either side of the urn and lit the candles.

She turned off the dining-room light, and suddenly twisted, writhing shadows danced on the walls. I moved closer to Avery, but love was not the reason.

"Nobody told me about seances," I muttered. I had an entirely uncharacteristic urge to wash the dishes. It was one thing to read about spirits and ghosts in a magazine, but I really didn't like the idea of inviting them to visit.

The thunder rumbled, and the first spatters of rain hit the windows. I'd barely begun to relax in this mausoleum in broad daylight. At night, with candles and thunder and Edmund's ashes it was a setting for *Friday the 13th Part Twelve*.

Why don't people ever hold seances in the daytime?

"Come sit down, Holly," Birdie said. "Maybe someone will have a message for you."

The only message I wanted to receive was, "Come back home, Holly, we're rich again."

"Nervous?" asked Avery.

I nodded. "I used to crawl under my chair at puppet shows."

"There's nothing to be afraid of," Blossom said. "Sit down, you two, and let's get started."

Avery and I took seats side by side. Blossom directed us to join hands and make an "unbreakable circle of faith."

At least I'd get to hold Avery's hand. And there was a shaft of light coming from the kitchen, so it wasn't completely dark.

Avery's hand was cool and pleasantly strong. I hoped that mine wouldn't start getting damp as I got more and more tense.

I avoided looking at Edmund's urn. Maybe if I closed my eyes—

But when Blossom started to speak they flew open. Her voice became deeper and more rhythmic, as if she were chanting a magic spell. "We have lit the seven mystic candles. Come to us from beyond the threshold of life and death . . ."

She swayed back and forth, as if she were about to lose consciousness, but she held onto Birdie's hand all the time. Her eyes closed, and her body moved as if she had no control over it.

There was a tremendous thunderclap, and the room was momentarily white with light. I shrieked and squeezed both of the hands I was holding. Avery squeezed back, but I was too jumpy to appreciate it.

Birdie let out a soft, "Ouch." I'd forgotten about her arthritis.

"Don't worry," Avery said. "We have a lightning rod."

"It's not just the lightning."

"Shh!" said Birdie.

"Edmund, my beloved, are you with us tonight?" Blossom cocked her head to one side. For a moment nothing happened. I told myself that I was lucky to be holding hands with Avery, and that I would never have had this chance without the seance. I told myself this was all superstitious nonsense.

"Yes, Edmund," Blossom said abruptly. "We have a new girl here."

I shot Avery a look of panic. I didn't want to be here, let alone be a topic of discussion from beyond the grave.

Avery smiled at me and then, very deliberately, winked.

"Do you have any message for our new companion?"

We waited in silence. I wished I were waiting in Mexico.

"She should learn how to fix the car . . . yes . . . she should use her salary wisely . . . yes, it is rather high, but—"

Avery bit his lip. He was struggling not to laugh.

"Is Archie there?" Birdie asked eagerly. "Does he have a message for me?"

The rain pelted the house like a shower of nails hitting the roof.

"Yes," Blossom said, in the same sing-song voice. "Archie wants you to learn Esperanto. Edmund is teaching him and Archie wants you to learn it too, so we can all speak it when we are together again."

Avery raised his eyebrows dramatically and rolled his eyes. There was no doubting what his message was. He was telling me he didn't believe a bit of this.

Then why did he go along with it? Was it easier to humor the two old ladies than to argue mystical philosophies?

Another thunderclap. The kitchen light went off for a few seconds and then came back on. A moment later it flickered off again, and stayed off. There was no light at all now except for the sputtering candles. One of the candles next to Edmund's urn suddenly went out for no reason I could see.

Avery leaned toward me. "At least we're prepared for a power failure," he whispered.

"But I *can't* learn Esperanto," Birdie said. She and Blossom ignored the sudden darkness. "I have no head for languages."

"Archie says you must try," Blossom went on.

"You always say that."

"Archie says it," Blossom said.

"Does he say anything about my memoirs?"

"He says," Blossom began, "that you should not live in the past—"

"You always say that too!" Birdie snapped. "I wish you'd say something that I wanted to hear."

I wished the lights would come back on.

"It's Archie's message," Blossom said. "Don't blame me for what Archie says. He loves you, you know. He wants you to be happy in this world until it's time to go to his."

Birdie said, "Ahh," and smiled contentedly.

Lit by a candle, Blossom's face looked flat and elongated. I thought of the Wicked Witch of the West, although Blossom didn't look quite that wicked.

It seemed strange that all the messages from beyond supported Blossom's domination of the household. One explanation might be, of course, that Blossom was faking. But I could hardly believe that. No one as direct as Blossom could be such a good actress. Where would she have gotten the practice?

Was she really communicating with the dead? Or did she only think she was? I didn't like either option. Crazy or creepy was not much of a choice.

"Good-bye, Edmund," she said. "We'll speak to you next week."

Not with me around.

The lights flashed back on again. I breathed a sigh of relief. Even if spirits still lurked around the dining-room table, the setting was nowhere near as spooky with the lights on.

Blossom was silent for a moment, her head slumped on her chest as if she had fallen asleep in her chair.

I looked questioningly at Avery. He shrugged. I'd have to get a chance to speak to him alone. Maybe he would be able to explain this away.

Blossom's eyes snapped open. She touched her hand to her curls. "Good," she said brightly. "Now let's play *keros*."

8

Yes, I was eager to go to the beach with Avery. No, I was not eager to go to the beach with Avery and his aunts. They packed baskets of food and supplies as if we were going on safari, and I had a frightening premonition that their bathing suits would have long skirts and black stockings.

But the choice was simply Avery or no Avery, so I got into a bathing suit and a T-shirt and helped to stow the baskets and bags in the hearse.

Even though it was only ten o'clock, there was a line of cars on Harmony Hill Road making slow progress toward the beach.

From the crest at the fork in the road we could see that the shorefront was already dotted with blankets and bathers. The air was cool and crisp after last night's thunderstorm. It was a perfect day for sailing.

I remembered my boating date with Pete, but it was

impossible to imagine sailing with Pete while Avery was sitting next to me.

Pete was scraping the bottom of a rowboat as we drove into the parking lot. He waved and headed toward us as Avery and I got out of the car.

"Hi, Pete," Avery said. "I guess it's officially summer."

Pete offered his hand to help Blossom out of the car, and I reached in to Birdie.

"As usual, you ladies packed enough equipment to spend six months on a desert island," he said.

"It's best to be prepared," Blossom said. "The *maro aero* gives one a hearty *apetito*."

Pete and I started to unpack the hearse. Our hands met in the middle of the backseat as we both reached for the same basket. His face lit up with pleasure, as if he was surprised to find me near him.

"I'm really looking forward to Tuesday," he said.

"Me too," I said hurriedly. "See you then." I wasn't interested in Tuesday. Avery was here today.

The parking lot was filling up as we trooped to the beach carrying two baskets of food, three large canvas bags, a pile of towels, and several blankets. We made quite a parade, the four of us and our gear. I was glad that I didn't know anybody on Harmony Island, because I felt extremely self-conscious in this caravan.

Unfortunately, I did know Chandra Gaines, who looked up as we marched past her blanket. She was stylishly seminaked in her extremely brief white bathing suit. She leaned on one elbow and pulled off her sunglasses, the better to stare at us.

She tapped her glasses against her lips and raised

one eyebrow. "Hi, Avery," she purred. "I've missed you."

Good grief. I thought she was after Pete. Why was she coming on to Avery? Or did she do this regularly, with every man she met? And why did she have to be so thin?

"Hi," Avery said. "Is your father here too?"

She shook her head. "He's in Brazil. I'm all alone."

I hope you stay that way, I thought. Better yet, go visit your father.

"Let's get a spot near the water," Blossom said. "We won't have to walk so far. Come on, Avery." She didn't waste a glance at Chandra, who returned the favor.

"See you later," said Avery.

"I hope so." Her voice was silky. Suggestive. She put her sunglasses back on and stretched out on her towel. She was as subtle as Daffy Duck.

Blossom found a spot just above the tide line and we spread out our blankets. I was surprised that she wanted to be so near the water. I'd assumed that she and Birdie were too old to swim.

I looked around at our little group and sighed. I'd imagined this moment for days. Avery and I, alone on the beach, racing to the water, laughing and splashing each other as we plunged in. He would turn and gaze at me lovingly, then sweep me into his arms and press his lips to mine.

Blossom pulled off her cotton shift, revealing a turquoise bathing suit loud with pink roses. My fantasy had not included an old woman in a blue-and-pink bathing suit.

How could we race into the water if Blossom was

going to swim too? You couldn't say, "Race you! Last one in is a rotten egg." The woman had broken her hip, for heaven's sake.

She might need my help even to get into the water. I was supposed to take care of her, not race her.

Avery looked sensational in his black trunks—slim and tanned, with legs that were splendid from any angle. He pulled off his shirt. The top of him was sensational too.

It was awfully chilly. Birdie shivered. She was still in her slacks and shirt. She reached into a canvas bag and pulled out a sweater. "It's cold, Blossom," she said. "You'll freeze."

"I'll be fine," Blossom said.

But it *was* very chilly near the shoreline. There were few bathers in the water. A biting breeze cooled me much more than I needed to be cooled. I hesitated before pulling off my T-shirt. I hate cold water. At home we had a heated pool.

Forget home, I told myself. Forget heated pools. Reality was a stiff wind and cold water.

Reluctantly, I took off my shirt, which, sadly, bared my fat thighs. There were a few extra pounds on me here and there, but *there* I needed heavy-duty liposuction.

But Avery didn't seem the least bit interested in my thighs. My bathing suit was more modest than Chandra's, but I had more to be modest about. If this were a contest—and it might be—I should never have entered the swimsuit competition.

Avery held out his arm to Blossom. "May I escort you into the ocean, madam?"

67

He was so cute. I couldn't blame him for not dashing down to the water with me, as he did in my fantasy. What a kind, thoughtful, devoted nephew he was. Great husband material.

Birdie tied a paisley scarf around her head. Maybe I ought to just sit on the blanket and wait for Avery and Blossom to turn blue and rejoin us.

But if I couldn't run into the bay with Avery, I could at least walk with him, so I boldly took his other arm.

"May I, sir?" I asked.

"My pleasure, mademoiselle." Even Blossom cracked a smile at that.

We walked slowly toward the water, joined together like unidentical Siamese triplets. We stuck our toes into the surf. One of us gasped as her toes instantly froze. It wasn't Blossom.

"Birdie's right," Avery said. He shivered. "Maybe you shouldn't go in today."

But Blossom had already let go of his arm and was wading ahead of us. "Very refreshing," she said. "But you have to take the plunge. It will be *agrabla* once you get all the way in."

"F-f-full of grapes?" My teeth chattered.

"Pleasant," Blossom translated.

I clung to Avery's arm as he waded toward Blossom, who was now up to her knees in water. My breath was coming in gasps. I tried not to shriek as my body turned to ice.

I didn't want Avery to think I wasn't physically fit. He was in great shape, and I was sure that he'd want the mother of his children to be hale and hardy.

I closed my eyes and clutched Avery until everything below my waist was numb.

Blossom must be made of leather.

"I'm going all the way in," Avery said. "Want to come?"

No, I wanted to die. Burning in hell sounded tempting. But here was my fantasy. We had to run into the water together and splash playfully before we kissed. How could I pass up this magic moment?

"Sure," I said.

"Yow!" He flung himself into the bay.

I threw myself in after him.

He came up for a breath, clutched his shoulders, said, "Wow, it's cold, isn't it?" and swam away. Without me. Without splashing me, without kissing me, without doing *anything* with me.

As I whimpered and shivered, I could see Blossom, already far out, swimming like a dolphin. Maybe she couldn't walk very well, but she didn't limp in the water.

Bitterly disappointed and definitely on the verge of pneumonia, I sloshed out of the water and went back to our blankets.

Birdie looked up from her book, *Your Lucky Life Numbers.* "You poor thing. You're almost blue with cold." She handed me a towel, and I dried myself off as fast as I could.

"Do you want a sweater?" she asked.

"No," I said. "I want a f-f-fur p-parka."

The chill air and my blue skin gave me an excuse to put my shirt back on and camouflage my thighs. Avery came out of the water shuddering and slapping his arms across his chest.

"Blossom didn't want to come out yet," he said. He toweled himself off. "She'll signal when she needs help."

What kind of help would she need? The woman swam like a fish.

Avery pulled his shirt back on and stretched out onto a blanket. "Keep an eye out for Blossom," he said. "I'm going to catch a few z's."

Birdie patted his knee and picked up her book. I wished I had a book. Or his knee. I wished I had thin thighs. I wished I were still rich.

"Yoo-hoo!" Blossom waved. She stood waist high in the water. I supposed she needed help getting out. Avery didn't lift his head. I would have to battle through the frigid waves again.

I gave a preliminary shiver as I pulled off my shirt. I tried to steel myself for the second arctic shock. I headed for the water and threw myself in.

They didn't pay me enough for this job.

Lunch consisted of leftover nutburgers (Don't I ever get a break?), Swiss cheese sandwiches, and potato salad. If sea air does give one a hearty appetite, it isn't for nutburgers.

I was gathering the remains of lunch to dump in a trash can, when Avery said, "I feel like a beer."

"I'm sorry," Blossom said. "I didn't bring any. I completely forgot about the beer."

"That's okay," he said. "I'll get one at Pete's. I wouldn't mind a little walk."

I jumped up. "I feel like one too."

"You drink?" Blossom fixed me with a steely gaze.

"No, I just meant I'm thirsty too. I want a Coke."

"I'll get it for you," Avery offered. "Regular or diet?"

He *had* noticed my thighs.

"I'll go with you," I said. "I can use some exercise." Particularly around my thighs.

At last! Alone with Avery. I walked very slowly, to make our intimate occasion last as long as possible. Meanwhile I tried to think of something to say to him.

"You're right. This *is* a nice beach. The water's awfully cold though."

"The kids congregate here all summer," he said. I could see there were knots of "kids" here and there along the curve of the water, but I didn't have the slightest interest in any of them. And I wished Avery would stop thinking of me as a kid.

"Have you met anyone?" he asked.

"Just Pete. And Chandra Gaines." I hoped my disgust was obvious.

"Oh, Chandra." There was no disgust in his voice. "Isn't she something? Boy, if I were a few years younger . . ."

Good grief. Who would have suspected he would have such rotten taste in women? I mean, I thought Chandra was something too, but it was certainly not the same something he meant.

How disillusioning. For the moment I felt paralyzed. I didn't have the strength to face this shock.

Here I am, taking care of two old ladies in total isolation, without air-conditioning, VCR, or any modern conveniences, working like a peon because I was deeply in love with this man, and he thought Chandra Gaines was *something*?

"Quite a body she's got," he added. How crude.

But I had to admit she had thin thighs. I wanted to cry.

Pete was waiting on a couple of little kids who were buying night crawlers when we went into the bait store. He looked up as we walked in and he beamed at me.

"I think he likes you," Avery said. I didn't want to hear that. This was terrible. Everything was upside-down. Pete liked me, but I didn't want a romantic relationship with him. Avery admired Chandra for shallow, superficial qualities like a terrific body and thin thighs, and Chandra was probably trying to seduce both of them.

The kids tromped out, waving their bait buckets at each other. "EEYEW! Look at those suckers!"

I tried to return Pete's smile, but I didn't have much smile left in me.

He and Avery chatted about motorboats or something, while Pete pulled soda cans from the ice chest. I didn't pay much attention.

When I looked up, Pete was gazing at me, apparently waiting for me to respond to something I hadn't heard.

"How do you like the beach?" he asked.

"Oh, nice. Water's cold."

"But it's a great day for sailing. I hope it's this nice on Tuesday. I'm going to take Holly out," he told Avery.

"Great. I think I'll come down tomorrow and rent a

powerboat. My aunts probably won't want to come so I'll only need a two-seater."

"I'll save something for you," Pete promised.

Avery paid for two beers and three cans of soda. He handed me the Diet Coke. "Why don't you stay and talk to Pete a while?" he suggested. "You haven't had a moment off since I got here."

Why was he trying to get rid of me? So he could go back to the beach and ogle Chandra without hurting my feelings?

"Yeah, stay," Pete urged. "It's pretty quiet now. My father's out on the dock, and I want you to meet him."

"Well, I really—"

The door flew open and Chandra slinked inside. She was wearing a sheer lace jacket over her nearly nonexistent bikini. Pete's Adam's apple jumped.

"Hi, Pete," she cooed. "Hi, Avery. Give me a Diet Coke, Pete."

She turned to Avery, who was juggling two bottles of beer and three cans of soda. "Wait a minute and I'll help you with those."

"Thanks," he said.

"You don't have to help—" I began. But neither of them was listening.

"So when's your father getting back from Brazil?" Avery asked her.

"In a week or so. He's not sure." She lowered her eyelids and fluttered her lashes. "But I'm really lonely."

Maybe that stuff would work on a boy like Pete, I told myself. But Avery was too mature and sophisticated to be deceived.

"Why don't you come over and visit Holly?" he said. "You two are about the same age."

We both stared at him as if he were crazy. Then Chandra shrugged. "Well, if you're going to be there . . ."

"Till Monday," he said.

Pete gave her a can of Diet Coke. "I'll pay you later," she said. "I forgot my wallet. Come on, Avery." She took two cans from him, and he opened the door for her. She wiggled out of the store as if her hips had a life of their own.

Pete stared at the empty doorway a good minute after she was gone. Finally he remembered that I was still there. "Is anything wrong? You look a little down."

What could be wrong? Merely that Chandra had wrangled an invitation out of Avery, which meant that not only would I have to share him with Blossom and Birdie, but with a girl he thought was "really something."

It was hard to look cheerful.

Pete came from behind the counter and put his arm around my shoulder. "What's the matter?"

"It's kind of personal." I couldn't admit to him that I was hopelessly in love with Avery, or that I had wild fantasies of marrying him for his money. As I thought about it now, it sounded ridiculous.

The best thing I could do would be to get off that island and find another job. Put all of them behind me—Chandra, Avery, Blossom . . .

Sure. And where would I ever find another job that paid eight dollars an hour? If I wasn't going to marry money I'd have to earn it.

A short, stocky man, with thinning blond hair the

same color as Pete's, pushed the door open. "Pete, I need some— Oh, hi." He grinned at me, as if he knew a secret. Pete squeezed my shoulder. "This is my father," he said. "Dad, this is the girl I told you about."

Why did he tell his father about me? What was there to tell? I shouldn't let him think—

"Hi, Holly. Nice to meet you. Pete, sorry to interrupt you, but I need some help with that Boston Whaler."

"That's okay," I said. "I was just leaving anyway."

"Will you be coming to the beach tomorrow?" Pete asked.

"I don't know."

"But I'll see you Tuesday, right?"

"I guess so."

I really didn't care.

9

Sunday morning at 9:37 Avery smiled at me and said, "Would you like to go out with me?"

I nearly dropped my toast. "Sure! I'd love to."

"I mean, in the boat."

A two-seater. Just Avery and me! That was as good as a regular date. He looked so nautical. Spiffy blue-and-white shirt and blue shorts with little anchors on the pockets.

"You bet!" I said. "I love boats."

I wished I had a great-looking boating outfit to put on.

"I invited Chandra to come along," he said.

NO! I couldn't stand it. How much more suffering could he inflict on me before I cracked completely?

Where's she going to sit? on your lap? But I didn't say it out loud. It was his rented boat and his lap, after all.

"She said she couldn't come." He didn't look too disappointed. "After I told her I was going to ask you too."

"Good," said Birdie, who was hanging on every word.

"That child is a disgrace," Blossom said. "She was a spoiled brat ten years ago, when her family started summering here, and she's a spoiled brat now."

Way to go, Blossom!

"Will you two be okay on your own?" he asked.

"We've been on our own for quite a while," Blossom reminded him.

"And you don't want to hang around us old ladies all weekend," Birdie added.

"I love to hang around with old ladies," Avery protested. He really was cute.

"Besides," Blossom said, "this is Holly's day off."

"It is?" Nobody had told me about it.

"Sundays," Avery said. "You have to have some time of your own. Didn't we talk about that?"

"Don't you want to visit your family?" Birdie asked. "You never speak of them."

"If you'd rather go off the island today, that's okay," Avery said.

"No, no," I said quickly. "Maybe next week."

Blossom packed us a lunch that consisted almost entirely of leftovers from last night's dinner—lentil salad and tofu custard, which were bad enough before they were recycled.

On the bright side, I would probably lose weight on this peculiar diet.

By ten o'clock we were on our way and my life was worth living again. Avery *did* want to be with me. And more than he wanted to be with Chandra. Otherwise he would have gone boating alone with her and never asked me to come along.

My fantasy wasn't an impossible dream after all. Just because Avery thought Chandra was "something," it didn't mean that she was something he wanted.

Progress on Harmony Hill Road was slow. We were in the middle of a progression of cars that was more traffic than I'd seen since I'd been there. I was grateful that Avery had offered to drive.

"Don't you feel funny," I asked, "driving a hearse?"

"No. I learned to drive in this car. It's a little eccentric, but then, so are my aunts."

I cleared my throat. "Speaking of eccentric," I began, "what did you think of that seance?"

He chuckled.

"I mean, Blossom really seemed to be in a trance."

"Maybe she was."

"But it was so eerie. Do you think she was really talking to Edmund?"

"She's really talking to him," Avery said. "What we don't know is whether he's talking back."

"But, I mean, you didn't seem to take it too seriously."

"It's harmless," he said. "And it makes them happy. After all, who are they hurting?"

Now I knew that Blossom wasn't faking. Which left only two possibilities, and I didn't like either of them. Either she was nuts or she was communicating with the other world.

We turned right down Harmony Hill. I could see the dock. The ferry was just chugging in, and there were a number of people lined up in the boatyard.

For a moment it seemed like a painting—the sun-bathers on the beach, the sailors, the little kids clustered by the shoreline—from this distance every element seemed frozen in time. The image of the perfect summer.

As if he knew what I was thinking, Avery said, "No matter how many times I come here, I never get tired of it."

"It's lovely," I agreed. It would be even lovelier if I were here as a guest rather than an employee. But then, anyplace would be lovelier if I weren't an employee.

We parked behind the store, and Avery pulled the basket of food out of the car. "Did you bring a hat?" he asked.

"No, I never thought of it."

"You can get one at Lou's." He pointed to the store. "Lou is Pete's father."

People milled around the dock, fitting orange life jackets on little kids, slipping mooring lines from their stanchions, stowing gear in their boats.

Pete and his father were at the shoreline, looking as if they needed to be six people instead of two. Pete saw us and waved. He said something to his father, who also waved at us.

"I've saved a neat boat for you," Pete shouted as he came toward us, "the *Mighty Mako*." He pointed to a red motorboat bobbing gently next to the dock.

"Great," said Avery. "We have to get Holly a hat, and we're all set."

Had his voice gotten a touch softer as he said my name, or was it just my imagination?

"Do you need one too?" Pete asked Avery. Avery pulled a captain's hat from the basket and set it on his head. He looked positively dashing.

"What kind of hat do you want?" Pete asked me.

A cheap one, I nearly said. "Just your basic hat. Nothing fancy."

We went into the store, and Pete pointed to a rack of hats in the corner. "Captain's, sailor's, brim, no brim, fishing, straw—"

"Too many choices," I said.

He snapped his fingers as if he'd had an inspiration. "I have just the hat for you." He pulled a white sailor cap from the rack. On top of it was a small bunch of red bead cherries. On the brim, in red embroidery, was stitched Life is just a bowl of . . .

He plopped it on my head.

"It's *you*," he said.

"You're right," I agreed. "The story of my life." How ironic. "How do I look?"

He pointed toward a little mirror on the shelf next to the hat rack. "You look cute," he said. His voice definitely got softer.

I did look cute. It was a cute hat. The message was so inappropriate that it made the hat even cuter.

"I'll take it. How much is it?"

He shook his head. "It's a present. Wear it for me on Tuesday."

"Tuesday!" I clapped my hand to my forehead. "I forgot about Tuesday."

He looked crushed. "You forgot about our date?"

"Today is my day off," I explained. "But I only found that out today."

"It doesn't have to be the whole day," he said. "Even a couple of hours would be nice."

"I'll ask," I promised. "And if I can't this week, maybe we could go sailing next week." I felt a little guilty that I wasn't nearly as upset over this as Pete was. But how could I help it if my heart had chosen Avery?

"I'd better get back to the dock," he said glumly.

Avery already had the engine idling as I got into the boat. The only thing I don't like about boats is getting in and out of them. But Avery's hand held mine firmly, and for the first time I experienced how pleasant getting into (or out of) a boat could be.

A man in a small Sailfish next to us gestured at Avery. "Go ahead," he said. "I'll wait till you're out."

"Thanks." Avery steered me into the seat next to the wheel and untied the rope that tethered the boat to the dock. He wobbled back to the wheel.

"Here we go!"

"Yikes!" We zoomed away from the dock so fast that I grabbed hold of the seat with one hand and tried to hold onto my hat with the other.

I managed to stay in the boat, but my hat didn't, and the last I saw of it, it was upside-down in the water and getting smaller.

Avery maneuvered around the boats heading outward. I thought he was going awfully fast, considering the traffic, so I didn't want to say anything about my hat that would distract him.

He was obviously a skillful boater—at least, we didn't hit anybody—and the speed was exhilarating. Especially after life with Blossom and Birdie.

I wondered if Avery was one of those playboys who drive cars too fast and take up with loose women who get him into messes that always embarrass their families. Though I couldn't think of anything Avery could do that would alienate his aunts. But if he did, after we were married I would reform him.

We passed the dock traffic and headed out into the bay. Avery tried to shout something at me over the noise of the engine, but I couldn't hear what it was. He put his lips next to my ear, and I was so startled at feeling his breath on my cheek that I didn't hear what he said.

He slowed the boat. The roar of the engine diminished somewhat.

"What happened to your hat?"

"Gone with the wind," I answered.

"You'd better take mine." He pulled off his hat and positioned it on my head. His fingers brushed my hair lightly, and I didn't move or breathe, wishing that this moment could last forever.

"There's a lot of glare off the water," he said.

The inside of the hatband was still warm from his head. It was as if he had thrown me a kiss.

The boat slowed to a steady *putt putt*. Avery kept one finger on the steering wheel. "Have you ever driven one of these?"

"My friends would let me steer once in a while, but I've never really driven one."

"If you're going to live here you ought to learn. Let's try it. We have to change places."

"Uh oh," I said.

"Just put your legs over mine and I'll slide underneath. Watch out for the gear shift."

We changed places almost simultaneously, so for a second or two I was actually sitting on Avery's lap. It was a miracle we didn't capsize, but water-safety rules didn't interest me.

Taking the steering wheel was a distinct let-down after Avery's lap.

"Just keep a straight course," he said. "It's very easy. Like a car. Always look around to make sure your lane is clear. When you see other boats, you have plenty of time to determine their direction and speed."

Avery kept talking about boating, and as I steered I tuned out his list of instructions and imagined that he was saying something entirely different.

". . . that's why I didn't care whether you had references . . . I knew the moment I saw you . . ."

It was all just as I'd pictured it. I had come to Harmony Island and done laundry and dishes and memoir writing and hearse driving and sat next to a dead man's ashes, all so I could have this moment.

More boats followed us out into the bay, and Avery gripped his hand over mine on the steering wheel. I loved the firm feel of his hand on mine. He didn't realize that his touch was more likely to cause an accident than to prevent one.

"I think I'd better take the wheel again," he said.

Goody, I thought, I get to sit on his lap again. Only this time he kept his hand on the wheel and slid over my lap.

Avery revved the engine and neatly threaded his way through the traffic.

I let my hand dangle in the water and tilted Avery's cap down over one eye. I wondered if I looked as cute in Avery's cap as I had in the hat with the cherries.

I knew that it was unrealistic to expect Avery to be in love with me already, but couldn't he make some remark about my relative cuteness or congeniality?

"That's Pirates' Cove." He pointed. "We can have lunch there."

I pushed the cap back on my head and saw we were approaching a little spit of land in the middle of the bay. It was like a tiny private island, with just a few trees and reeds and tall marsh grass.

An old, decrepit piling, like the remains of a skeleton, jutted up at the bank. "We'll have to wade," Avery said. "Do you mind?"

I would rather wade with you than have my American Express card back, I thought.

"No," I answered. "I'm dressed for wading."

He turned off the engine and hopped out of the boat. He grabbed hold of the tie line and made his way to the piling. The water was up to his thighs, so I knew I wouldn't drown, and besides, anything that covered my thighs was welcome.

He hitched the rope with some kind of complicated sailor's knot and slogged back to the boat to get the lunch basket. I followed him out of the water, thinking that this was one of the most romantic settings I could imagine for a marriage proposal.

Silly, I told myself. This is a first date.

"We have the whole island to ourselves," he said. He couldn't possibly be as glad about that as I was.

Blossom had actually packed a tablecloth with the lunch, so I spread it out under a tree and began setting out the food.

"Next time," Avery said, spooning up some lentil salad, "we'll stop in town first and buy our own lunch."

Who cared about food? Even tofu custard tasted good with Avery beside me.

All right, it didn't taste good, but I didn't mind.

He leaned back against the tree trunk. "I used to come here when I was a kid. To be alone. I pretended this was my secret hiding place. But everyone with a boat knows Pirates' Cove."

"Did you like to be alone when you were a kid?" I asked. "You seem pretty sociable now."

"When I first came here, right after my parents died, I spent a lot of time alone. It was a long while before I felt secure again."

I knew what he meant. Even if he married me—even if his money rescued me and my family—I would never again feel as safe as I did when I was a child.

"Blossom and Birdie were wonderful. Blossom was kind of stern, but I knew she cared about me."

"How old were you when your parents died?"

"Nine. You know, they even played baseball with me."

"Your aunts?"

He nodded. "Uncle Edmund had just died that year. It must have been awfully tough on Blossom, but she never showed it."

"Did she hold seances then?"

He laughed. He leaned forward and tugged the cap down over my eyes. "How serious we're getting. This is a vacation."

"Not for me it isn't," I said, and instantly regretted it.

He pushed the cap back on my head. "I know." He studied my eyes for a moment, as if he were trying to see past the outer surface and into my soul. "I'm sure it's not the easiest job in the world."

He reached out and tilted my chin up with his hand. He's going to kiss me, I thought, and tried not to tremble as he moved closer.

I closed my eyes, and suddenly his hand was off my chin, and yanking the hat back down over my face.

"Enough seriousness," he said briskly. "The seances only started a year ago. And it's time for your second boating lesson."

I opened my eyes to see that he had already moved away from me and was cleaning up the debris from our lunch. I tried to send thought waves to him. You can kiss me if you want to. I won't mind.

But he didn't, and I guess he didn't catch my thought waves. My arms were heavy with disappointment as I folded up the tablecloth.

Maybe he thinks it's too soon, I told myself. Maybe he'll kiss me tomorrow. He could be worried about the difference in our ages. He doesn't realize that suffering has matured me.

My second and last boating lesson was turning right, left, and in a circle back toward Harmony Island. He didn't want to leave his aunts alone too long. He let me steer until we saw the ferry approaching the dock. Then we switched places again.

The thrill was definitely gone. I had hoped by now that we would have progressed further than split-second lap sitting.

Avery would be going back to the city tomorrow, and the longest weekend of the summer would be over with nothing to show for it, unless Avery forgot to take back his captain's hat.

He maneuvered the boat back to the pier and roped it to a piling.

Maybe he'll say something in the car, I thought. Maybe he'll stop the car and kiss me at the top of Harmony Hill.

But he didn't.

That night we watched as fireworks lit up the whole island. Even Blossom applauded some of the spectacular displays.

Pete sat on the beach with us, he and Avery trying to identify each type of firecracker as it went off. It was really quite a show.

If only I could have seen it alone with Avery, snuggled together with a blanket over our shoulders, ignoring the rest of the crowd on the beach, pretending that the fireworks were being performed for just the two of us.

I didn't even get to keep his hat.

10

I was so depressed. Avery was gone, and because of his visit, Blossom had saved me the laundry for Tuesday. I assumed that this meant my date with Pete would have to be cancelled, but it had never been a high priority.

Between washloads Birdie dictated more of her memoirs. We were just up to her whirlwind courtship and brief honeymoon when Blossom called me.

"Telephone, Holly. It's your sister."

"I didn't know you had a sister," Birdie said.

I ran down to the kitchen and Blossom handed me the receiver. "You didn't tell us you had a *fratino*." She made me feel like I should apologize for not mentioning Sloane.

Blossom left me alone in the kitchen.

"Holly," Sloane said, "why haven't you called? It's been almost two weeks."

"Oh, Sloane! I didn't realize how much I missed you

to punch something. "They're not home," I said. "They were going to leave when we finished talking."

I could have visited my father, but what would we talk about? The stock market? Laundry? His former company? My current job?

I didn't know if he was ready to deal with me one on one. And I didn't know if I could talk to him without mentioning money. I didn't want to hurt him.

Pete studied my face. He looked as unhappy as I felt. "Holly, I can't go sailing today, but we could go out for lunch."

"*Bono ideo!*" Blossom said.

"Just what you need," Birdie agreed. "And bring back a quart of pistachio ice cream."

"A pint," said Blossom. They were practically throwing me out of the house. Miserable as I felt, I was grateful for their concern.

"Okay." I couldn't work up too much enthusiasm for a hamburger at the Chat 'n' Nibble, but it would be a welcome change from walnut cutlets. "Let's go."

"Great!" said Pete. Either he was a lot more excited by this lunch than I was, or he was acting extra cheerful for my benefit.

"It's only ten-thirty though," I said. "I could do some more work on Birdie's memoirs before—"

"They're forty years old," Birdie said. "They'll wait another few hours."

"And practice fixing the butterfly *valvo*," Blossom said sternly.

How could I practice? I never learned in the first place.

Pete and I went outside to his truck.

"You still don't know how to fix that valve?"

"You were supposed to teach me," I reminded him.

"Okay, let's do it now."

"No, I'm too depressed to get my hands greasy. Let's do it when we get back and I'm in a good mood."

We got into the truck. "I came to tell you that I can't go sailing today after all," Pete said. "There's a lot of stuff to be cleaned up after the weekend."

"That's okay," I said. "Lunch will be a nice change of pace from split peas and sprouts."

"Would you like to walk around town and do some shopping?" he asked.

I nodded. "Shopping is one of my best things." I had to go back into the house to get my wallet.

"Don't forget the *valvo!*" Blossom shouted after me.

"Is there a bank in town?" I asked. Pete drove away from the house and onto Harmony Hill Road. I had two weeks pay in my wallet, and since I planned to save most of it, I might as well earn interest on the money.

"Two banks," Pete answered.

"Savings or commercial?" We might be poor, but I was still my father's daughter.

"What's the difference?"

"The savings banks usually pay a higher interest rate."

As we drove toward town I half expected Chandra to appear behind us in her Jaguar, honk loudly, and make a rude hand gesture as she passed us. Reckless driving and harassing me were her hobbies, after all.

But we got to town uneventfully, and Pete parked the truck in front of the Seamen's Savings Bank.

"I guess this is a savings bank," he said. "I never knew there was a difference."

The bank looked more like an early colonial house than a bank. It was very small inside and there were lines at the two tellers' windows.

A woman at a large desk gave me forms to fill out to open a savings account. She presented me with a blue ballpoint pen with Seamen's printed on it. "Your free gift," she said.

"I'd rather have another half percent interest," I said.

"I don't blame you," she said.

We went to stand in line so I could make my first deposit. "I'll be on this line," Pete said, "and you stand on the other. That way you can't pick the wrong line."

"Good idea."

There were five people in Pete's line and three in mine. My line moved steadily, but Pete's seemed stalled.

Then, just as I was one person away from the window, the sharply dressed man in front of me told the teller he wanted to deposit six hundred dollars. In pennies. Everyone behind me groaned.

Pete's line speeded up, and I eyed it, ready to make the switch. The woman in front of him handed the teller a check, and Chandra strolled into the bank.

My idea of hell—trapped in a small, enclosed space with Chandra Gaines.

Pete motioned for me to switch lines, but almost faster than the eye could see Chandra scooted in front of him. "You don't mind, do you, Pete?"

Taken by surprise, Pete just shrugged helplessly. My

teller had only reached 317 pennies, so if Chandra was not applying for a mortgage, her business shouldn't take too long.

"Come on, Holly," Pete said. "This line will still be faster."

I debated with myself if it were preferable to wait while the teller counted out 283 more pennies, or stand next to Chandra for thirty seconds.

It was a tough call. The man in front of me said, "When you finish the pennies we'll do the dimes."

My whole line moved over to the next window. I took my place in front of Pete. Chandra tucked a wad of bills into her white jumpsuit as I replaced her at the teller's window. She took Pete's arm and pulled him away from me so I couldn't hear what she was saying.

By the time I got my new bankbook stamped, Chandra's hand was welded to Pete's arm.

Maybe I was being unfair. After all, I hardly knew her. Maybe she just gave a bad first impression. Maybe underneath that prickly exterior lurked a truly nice person.

Nah.

I walked as slowly as possible toward Pete and Chandra, who were standing near the door. I hoped she would leave before I reached them. But she didn't. I determined to be as pleasant as I could. In the overall scheme of things, Chandra was very unimportant. Avery hadn't succumbed to her charms, and what Pete felt for her was none of my business.

"Hi, Chandra," I said pleasantly.

"Hi," she said pleasantly back. "Are you opening an account here?"

Relief spread all over Pete's face. Maybe because Chandra and I were not killing each other.

"You know," I said pleasantly, "every time I've seen you you've been wearing white. Do you always dress in white?"

"Yes," she said. "I know it's an affectation, but at least I never have to bother matching anything." Her eyes swept up and down my body. I was wearing a yellow T-shirt and faded denim shorts. When I'd dressed that morning I hadn't expected to be in a fashion competition.

"I guess you dress for comfort rather than style," she said pleasantly.

Pete winced.

"I mean, what's the point of dressing well to take care of two old ladies? As long as you're neat and clean that should be enough," she said pleasantly.

I cracked. "I have plenty of good clothes at home!" I said. "You should see my closets. They're *bulging* with clothes. *Expensive* clothes!"

My voice rose so high that people turned to stare at me. How could I have said anything that stupid, even if it was the truth? I sounded like a jealous seven-year-old.

Pete hustled us out of the bank, one hand on each of our backs.

I seethed with anger, not only because of what Chandra had said, but because I'd let her get to me. At least I didn't have to pretend to be pleasant anymore. My first impression had been right. She was poisonous.

"Where do you want to go now, Holly?" Pete asked nervously.

Devil's Island. The Australian outback. Ethiopia. As far away from Chandra as I could get.

"Holly wants to do some shopping," he explained.

"I can imagine," Chandra said.

I'm not going to say a word. Not one word.

"Would you like to uh"—he flashed me a look of desperation—"to come with us?"

She raised one eyebrow. "I think not."

Pete exhaled loudly, as if he had been holding his breath for the last ten minutes.

I took his arm possessively.

"We'd better get going," he said. "I don't have too much time."

I could almost hear Chandra gnashing her teeth. She managed a feeble smile. "Have a nice day," she said. But she didn't say it pleasantly.

II

Pete rested his hand lightly on my shoulder as we strolled down Main Street. I kept looking behind me to make sure Chandra wouldn't sneak up and chop Pete's hand off.

And his hand felt good. It was reassuring to know that he cared about me. Since April I had made myself a hermit, huddling in the house, alienating all my friends. I didn't want to talk to anyone, as if it were a shameful secret that we weren't rich anymore. I felt sorry for myself, but I guess I didn't really want anyone else to pity me.

We browsed through the bookstore. I had plenty of time to read in the evenings, and I'd kept fifty dollars in cash from my first two weeks salary.

Prominently displayed near the counter was a shelf of self-help books. In the center of the rack was a book called *Think and Grow Rich*.

"Hardy har har," I said sarcastically.

Pete picked up the book and began leafing through it. "You don't think this would work?"

"Trust me," I said. "I've been thinking about being rich for months, and I'm not one cent richer."

"But you are," he said. "You've got a job."

"Well, okay," I admitted, "I'm well paid. But I'm not rich."

"You haven't been working very long. It doesn't promise you'll get rich overnight."

"Why don't you buy it?" I asked.

"I don't need to get rich," he said. "I've got enough money and I'm doing what I like."

"I wish I could say that."

His voice grew soft. "I wish you could too." If I hadn't been absolutely sure of his feelings before, there was no doubt about them now. I could see them in his eyes, hear them in his voice. Again I wondered if I was being fair not telling him about Avery.

But his hand felt so comfortable and his voice was so sweet when he spoke to me. I needed a friend, and Avery hadn't even kissed me yet. There really wasn't anything to tell.

I picked out two Agatha Christie mysteries that I hadn't read yet. I paid for the books in cash—a new experience for me, considering the number of credit cards I used to have.

We were nearing the Chat 'n' Nibble when I asked Pete if he wanted to eat now. "I'm getting hungry from all this shopping."

"Sure," he said. He took my hand in his and we walked past the coffeeshop. Right past Chandra's Jaguar.

"We're not eating here?" I asked.

"Nope. We're going to the best restaurant on the island."

We turned off Main Street, and he pointed toward the end of the block. "The Harmony House. Opposite the fire station."

"But I'm not dressed for the best restaurant on the island," I protested. "Look at me."

"I'm looking. You're adorable."

"I'm *serious*."

"So am I," he said. "This is a very casual place. And they'll just be opening up. There won't be that many people there, and you won't scandalize them."

As soon as I stepped into the dimly lit restaurant I knew I was going to like it. The hostess greeted Pete by name and led us past the bar to a little garden in the back. The few people already there wore sports clothes, and it was quiet and cool and green.

I relaxed and examined the menu. There was a special of soft-shelled crabs, which I love. Pete ordered a steak sandwich.

The waiter left us alone and Pete leaned across the table toward me. He held out his hand. I put my hand in his. A smile lit up his whole face.

I've got to tell him the truth, I thought, before this goes any further.

"I don't know anything about you," he said. "You're still my mystery girl."

"My story is a long and sad one," I said.

"You told me that. I want to hear it anyway."

Suddenly, to my astonishment, words, sentences, paragraphs of my history began to spill from my lips. I was still talking when the waiter brought our salads.

Pete let go of my hand so I could pick up my fork, but I didn't need it because I was too busy talking to eat.

By the time I finished, bringing him as far as my first interview with the Brewsters, my mouth was dry. I told him the truth, and even though I didn't mention Avery, I felt a wonderful sense of relief, as if a boulder had been lifted from my chest.

"That's really tough," Pete said sympathetically. "It sounds like a Movie of the Week."

"Yeah," I agreed. "A true riches-to-rags saga."

My crabs arrived and I dug into them eagerly. They were delicious. Telling the truth had given me an enormous *apetito*.

"That was a great lunch," I said. "Everything was so good."

Pete nodded. "It was one of my top ten lunches. And it wasn't because of the food."

He left a small pile of bills on top of the lunch check. As we left the restaurant he put his arm around my waist.

"I wish I didn't have to go back to work," he said.

"Me too."

I meant that I didn't want to go back to Blossom and Birdie, but I could see that he thought I meant I didn't want him to go back to the boatyard.

He looked so pleased that I didn't have the heart to straighten it out. It was no big deal, I told myself. I *did* like him. And I'd just trusted him with the story of my life, which I didn't even want to tell Avery.

He tightened his arm around my waist and gave it a squeeze. I couldn't help feeling a preliminary tingle, the little shiver I got when I was attracted to someone. What was a little squeeze between friends? It's just a friendly hug. Nothing serious. I put my arm around him. After all, it was only polite to return his warm gesture.

Being squeezed and squeezing back took me past preliminary tingle right into rush of heated emotion. If I were not careful this would lead to serious kissing and hugging, and that would definitely give Pete the wrong impression about us.

"Holly? You want to come to the boatyard with me and watch me scrape hulls?"

I unwrapped my arm from his waist and tried to ignore how extremely tanned, blond, and muscular he was.

"A tempting invitation," I said, "but I've got to get back to the Brewsters."

He sighed melodramatically. "So near and yet so far."

We reached the truck, and he helped me climb into the front passenger seat. "I hope there's a major traffic screw-up on Harmony Hill," he said, climbing in beside me. "I hope it takes three hours to unscrew it."

But there wasn't. As we rode back to the house I kept sneaking peeks at his profile. I couldn't help it. I was still tingling.

As I said, I'd had a reasonably active social life B.P. (before poverty). I'd been going out with college boys since I was fourteen. Good-looking college boys. From Ivy League colleges.

If I was interested in a boy it didn't take very long to get him interested in me. To be entirely truthful, I'd pretty much had my pick of boyfriends. (B.P.)

And sitting next to Pete in the truck, I was still tingling.

What was so terrible about wanting to be loved? It's a natural human desire. I needed to feel close to somebody.

Pete drove very slowly. When we got to the top of Harmony Hill Road, where we could look down at the beach, he stopped the truck.

He reached for me, and I leaned toward him so he could put his arms around me. He kissed me until I felt like warm Jell-O.

"Better get going," he said finally. "I have hulls to scrape."

"And I have sheets to hang," I said.

"Oh, hang the sheets!" he said, and took me in his arms again.

Birdie must have been watching from the window for our return, because she had the front door open before I even got out of the truck.

"Did you have a good time?" she asked.

"I had a very good time." I smiled. She smiled back. I had the distinct impression that she knew exactly what I meant by "good time."

"Did you bring the ice cream?"

"Oops. I forgot."

Blossom, leaning on her cane, didn't look as jolly. "Did you learn how to—"

"Oh, no! I forgot that too."

"This is outrageous," she said. "The whole point of your being here is to help out in case of an emergency. And you haven't even taken a couple of minutes to learn

how to fix the car. What are you going to do if something happens to Birdie and you have to get her to a
doctor? Or what if something happened to me? Who'd
fix the car?"

"She could call Pete," Birdie suggested timidly.

"*I* could call Pete!" Blossom thundered. "We're not
paying her eight dollars an hour to call Pete."

"I'm sorry. I just forgot."

"You can't say we don't treat you well," Blossom
went on. "We did the laundry that you were supposed
to do so you could have some free time."

"I'm sorry. It just slipped my mind. I'll get Pete to
show me next time."

"*I* will show you *now*."

Her back was rigid, even as she limped. I followed
her out the back door at a respectful distance. I couldn't
blame her for being angry about the car, but it wasn't
fair for her to offer to do the laundry, and then remind
me of it afterward. And I *earned* my salary. Even if it
was high.

She opened the garage doors and climbed into the
hearse. She backed it out of the garage and pointed it
toward the road.

"Come here. Look under the hood." I looked under
the hood.

"This is the oil filter. You unscrew the nut on top of
it and take off the filter."

This sounded sort of familiar.

"See that pipe? The butterfly valve is inside the pipe.
It gets stuck closed and you have to wedge it open."

I knew I should pay attention to Blossom's demon-
stration, but I couldn't concentrate on auto mechanics

after half an hour of Pete's kisses. My eyes were on Blossom, but the rest of me was back in Pete's truck. I was still tingling.

There was no reason to tell Pete about Avery, I decided, even if he was becoming seriously attached to me. He wanted to kiss me, and I wanted to be kissed, so why not let him? There was a strong physical attraction between us. It was the most natural thing in the world to give in to it.

Blossom's sharp voice interrupted my tingling. "Now you do it."

Not surprisingly the only thing I'd heard of her directions was how to take off the oil filter.

"I will show you again," she said grimly. She pointed out the pipe and the valve, and how to wedge the valve open with a stick.

"Be sure to close the valve as soon as the engine starts. With the valve open there is some danger of fire."

How was I supposed to hold the valve open and start the car at the same time?

But I didn't ask. There would be someone around to start the car for me. If anything happened to one of the Brewster sisters, the other could start the car while I held the valve open.

Besides, I could always phone Pete.

12

That week Pete found a lot of reasons to come to the house. There was a warped wooden door that had to be sanded, a cracked window-pane to replace, and a loose shingle on the roof.

"Such a thoughtful boy," Blossom commented. Birdie and I giggled like co-conspirators.

Birdie always offered Pete something to eat and drink, usually prolonging his stay an hour past the time the repair took.

Blossom didn't seem to mind when we strolled out to his truck holding hands. Instead she asked Pete to drill me on fixing that stupid butterfly valve, because she was convinced that I hadn't been paying attention when she tried to show me how. If I never heard the words *butterfly* or *valve* again, I would be extremely grateful.

We took rags with us so we could clean the engine grease from our hands and not leave black stains on each other's clothes when we snuggled behind the garage.

With Pete dropping in every day, and Birdie encouraging him, my job became a lot more pleasant. We had reached Birdie's honeymoon in her memoirs, and she was having a hard time trying to decide how much to tell her readers.

"Everything's so explicit these days," she said. "I'm not sure the public would accept a book like mine without some sex in it."

She finally decided that since she couldn't dictate the events of her honeymoon to me without blushing and stammering, she would simply hint at wedded bliss and leave out the clinical details.

"Romance is more fulfilling than raw sex," she said. "Don't you think?"

How should I know? I hadn't had *that* much experience. "Definitely," I replied.

Blossom still made me feel that she didn't need me, no matter how many things she found for me to do. It was as if she was determined to get Avery's money's worth out of me, even if she had to make up chores to fill my day.

I told myself that she was just a crochety old lady who resented not being able to do all the things she used to do before she got old and broke her hip.

But I still couldn't like her any better. She was quick to criticize and slow with praise.

She still wanted me to learn Esperanto so I could converse with her, and she gave me a book about the language with a dictionary in the back. She told me to carry it around with me and look up words I didn't understand.

My motivation for learning Esperanto was zip. Especially when I found there were no swear words in the dictionary.

And then it was Friday, the day Avery would come. Blossom sent me to town with a long list, including, of course, seven white candles for the seance. I'd get to hold Avery's hand again.

Even nutburgers would taste good with Avery eating them next to me.

Well, not really good, but I could stand them.

I was just staggering out of the Superette with two bulging plastic shopping bags, when Chandra's Jaguar screamed to a stop right in front of the store. She vaulted out of the car and charged toward me.

She stuck a finger in my chest and said, very loudly, "Stay away from Pete."

That there were people going into and coming out of stores all around us didn't slow her down. Her face was red with anger, and shoppers gave us a wide berth as they passed us.

I didn't want to put down the shopping bags because they might spill, so I couldn't smack her finger away.

I moved backward. She moved toward me. She looked nearly hysterical and I wondered if she was capable of violence.

"Pete is *mine*," she said, jabbing me. "He's been mine since I was ten years old." Jab. "Every summer since I started coming here we've been together. I'm not going to let someone like *you* take him away from me." Jab.

"I'm not trying to take him away from you. I can't help it if he likes me."

And what did she mean "someone like *you?*"

"It's only because you're new here," she said. "He'll get tired of you and come back to me."

"Then what are you worried about?" I asked.

"I'm only here for the summer. I don't want to wait until he's tired of you. He wastes enough time as it is fixing things for those weirdos you baby-sit."

"Listen, Chandra, I've got ice cream melting—"

"No, you listen to me!" she screamed. I backed away from her, moving toward the hearse. I felt the stares of passersby burn into me. I focused on the sidewalk so I wouldn't have to see the stares. All I wanted to do was to get inside the car.

"I'm not going to let a cheap nothing like you screw up my summer! Stay away from him or I'm going to make you sorry you ever looked at him!"

She sounded like Joan Crawford.

I threw the shopping bags in the backseat of the car. Apples and plums spilled out and rolled around the seat.

I had to get away from her red, screaming face, and the audience we were drawing. Strolling shoppers pretended not to hear Chandra's tantrum, but you could have heard her in Pago Pago.

I jumped into the car, locked the door, breathed a sigh of release, and turned the key.

Chug, chug, cough.

Oh, God, not now.

I tried it again. Burp, burp, click. Nothing.

What timing. I leaned my head against the steering wheel. I wanted to throw a tantrum of my own. I had to get away from her. I had to get out of here. Even if I was sure I knew how to fix the valve, I'd have to do it with her screaming at me.

I couldn't picture asking her to help me out by starting the ignition, not unless I wanted to get run over.

When I raised my head, she was gone. I looked around to see the Jaguar peel out of its parking space and tear up Main Street.

What a horrible five minutes. I couldn't remember a more frightening experience, except for going broke. Chandra was a lot crazier than Blossom or Birdie.

I said a silent prayer that I would never see her again as long as I lived. Then I got out of the car and went to look for a pay phone to call Pete.

When I got back to the house, with melted ice cream, bruised fruit, and a crushed box of oat bran, Blossom and Birdie were so glum that Blossom didn't even complain about the condition of the groceries.

She didn't look at the food as I put it away. She didn't ask for the receipt. Even though *Divorce Court* was over, she didn't ask what had taken me so long.

She limped into the kitchen as I was folding up bags.

"Make some *lunco*," she said. She didn't sound a bit hungry. "And a pot of *teo*."

"Is something wrong?" I asked.

"Our nephew will not be coming this weekend."

"Not coming! But I thought he always—" This wasn't fair. He was supposed to be here every weekend.

"Why not?" I asked.

"Maybe he had something he wanted to do more," Blossom said. "Or maybe he thinks we don't need him now that you're here." It was clear from her tone of voice that she believed it was my fault that Avery wasn't coming. She was probably right.

Avery had said he might skip a few weekends now that I was taking care of his aunts. But already? I was the reason he wasn't coming, and he was the reason I was here in the first place. If Blossom resented me before, she must hate me now. Even Birdie might not be too crazy about me after this. Which meant that I might not have this job much longer.

Which meant I would never see Avery again. But if he didn't visit, I wouldn't see him either.

I had no *apetito* for the cream-cheese-and-walnut sandwiches I prepared. I spread out the lunch on the kitchen table and went upstairs to my room.

I wanted to kick something. I wanted to kick someone. Harmony—what a name for this place. I'd met four people here and two of them hated me. Terrific feeling. But their hatred didn't distract me from the disappointment about Avery.

I had anticipated his visit since Monday night, the moment after he left. I was sure that we would go out to Pirates' Cove again this weekend. But even if we only went to the beach with the aunts, we could still talk. I wanted to learn more about him. I didn't even know what he did for a living.

I wanted to tell him how I felt about him. I wanted to hear how he felt about me. I wouldn't go into my life story yet, but there were other aspects to me than poverty.

I closed the door to my yellow, green, and orange room. I lay back on the bed and stared at the ceiling. I tried to decide whether I was more sad than angry, or more angry than sad.

I punched my pillow. Hard. Then I grabbed it to my chest and started to cry.

I decided I was very angry *and* very sad.

When you come to the end of a rotten day there is not much you can do to make yourself feel better except go to sleep and wait for tomorrow.

My day as a companion unofficially ended after I cleared away the dinner dishes. That night, as I wiped the last plate, I was looking forward to eight hours of unconsciousness. I couldn't wait to get back to my ugly room, to turn out the lights, to turn off my mind, to sleep for as long as possible.

"Get the candles, Holly," Blossom said. "I'll get Edmund's urn."

Oh, no. I'd had enough for one day. I had cooked and cleaned and shopped and washed dishes and had been humiliated in public. To top it all off, I had to face the weekend without Avery. The last thing I needed was a rerun of *The Twilight Zone.*

I took the candles from the china cabinet and lay them down on the table.

"I'll be in my room," I said. "Seances are not me."

"But we need you," Birdie said. "It's always better with three people."

"What did you do before I came?"

"Avery was usually here," Blossom said. "I would like you to stay. A third person increases the field of *energio*."

Birdie rubbed her hands together. Her fingers were crooked and her knuckles were red. She couldn't even clasp her hands together. "Please stay, Holly."

How could I refuse? She was old, she was crippled with pain, and all she asked of me was to help her with her memoirs.

"Okay." It was against my better judgment, but . . . "I'll stay."

Blossom said, "Thank you. We appreciate it."

I nearly fainted.

She lit the candles and sat down at the table. Birdie and I sat on either side of Blossom. Blossom closed her eyes and began to chant.

"We have lit the seven candles and are joined in an unbreakable circle of faith. Come to us . . . come to us . . . cross the bridge between our worlds. Speak to us from beyond the threshold of life and death."

She began to sway back and forth, her eyes closed, her hand loosely gripping mine.

Don't come, I thought. Don't come. Without Avery there to hold my hand and wink, this was even more scary than it had been the first time.

Blossom began to rock sideways, but she had hardly begun when her eyes opened and she looked around the room as if she expected someone to materialize.

"Edmund, is that you?"

Now I looked around the room, searching the shadows in the corners for signs of afterlife.

"What's wrong?" Blossom asked someone.

Birdie's mouth opened as if she was getting ready to scream. She looked tensely from Blossom to the urn to me.

"Major changes?" Blossom asked. "Danger?"

Birdie gasped. Blossom's voice was slow, somber. She didn't sound afraid, but I was afraid enough for all of us.

I wanted very badly to break the unbreakable circle of faith, but I didn't know what would happen if I did. Would evil spirits invade the seance and take over Blossom's body? Would Birdie really panic and have a heart attack?

"Blossom," Birdie whispered.

"*Shhh.* Go on, Edmund. A sudden accident? An illness? When? Edmund, I can hardly hear you."

I closed my eyes so I couldn't see the silhouettes writhing on the walls, but I was even more frightened with my eyes closed. Was a spirit sneaking up behind me?

I told myself that was nonsense, but I kept my eyes open anyway.

"Yes, all right. We'll be prepared. Yes, she has learned how to fix the car. Don't worry, Edmund. We'll be very careful."

"Is Archie there?" Birdie whispered.

Blossom listened. "Archie's here too. He loves you, but he doesn't want you to cross the bridge before your time. He says . . . I can't hear too well."

Birdie's eyes filled with tears. "I love you too, Archie."

"*Adiau* for now," Blossom said. She lowered her head

and let go of my hand. I realized I'd been holding my breath.

She lifted her head and looked around. "Well," she said crisply, "I didn't expect that."

"What do you suppose will happen?" Birdie asked.

Blossom shrugged. "Edmund said if we were alert to the danger—or the changes, I couldn't hear very well—if we were alert, the worst wouldn't happen."

"The worst?" I felt a chill. "You mean—"

"So, Holly, I hope you are *absolutely sure* you know how to fix the *valvo?*"

13

Saturday morning we went to the beach. I crept along at nine miles an hour, which drove Blossom crazy.

"We'll never get to the *marbordo* at this rate."

"Better safe than sorry," Birdie said.

"Nervous Nellies," Blossom muttered.

The *marbordo* was pretty busy, but without Avery things were dull and time dragged.

I was half drowsing when a shadow fell across my face.

"Ahh." It was Pete. "Sleeping Beauty."

I opened my eyes. "Hi, Prince Charming."

"You're not supposed to wake up until he kisses you," Birdie scolded.

"Want to try it again from the beginning?" Pete asked. "I'm game if you are."

"I'm too old for fairy tales." Which I realized was not

true the instant I said it. I *was* trying to write my own version of Cinderella, with Avery as my handsome prince.

"Okay, then how about a party? Tonight. You don't know anyone here except me."

"And you-know-who," I said.

"That's a wonderful idea," Birdie said. "Don't you think so, Blossom? Holly ought to make some friends her own age."

Blossom looked up briefly from her book, a paperback with a gory cover and a gruesome title. "Yes," she said, and went back to reading.

"It's unanimous," Pete said. "I'll pick you up at eight-thirty."

"Wait a minute! I didn't vote yet," I said. "Will you-know-who be there?"

"I don't know. What's the difference?"

"Are you kidding? After yesterday I'm afraid to be on the same planet with her, let alone the same party."

"You can't shut yourself in and hide from her all the time," he said.

"Who says I can't? I just have to avoid her until the summer is over."

"That's crazy," Pete said. "After what you've been through, this is baby stuff."

"Been through?" I could almost see Birdie's ears prick up. "Been through what?"

"Just some family problems," I said.

Birdie nodded. "I thought so. Now, dear, we want you to forget everything for a while and have some fun. You shouldn't have to be cooped up with two old ladies all the time. Right, Blossom?"

"That's what we pay her for," Blossom said, not even looking up from her book.

Her remark worked like reverse psychology on me.

"Okay, I'll go."

Pete and Birdie smiled triumphantly, as if they had won a great victory. Blossom wet her index finger with her tongue and turned a page.

I should have gone shopping. I didn't have a thing to wear. I had beach stuff, clothes to do laundry in, and pajamas.

"You look great," Pete said as I walked downstairs. I was wearing a black tube top and shorts that looked sort of like a miniskirt.

"I should have bought something," I said. "Are any of the stores still open?"

"Not now. But you really look great. Don't you think so, Mrs. Brewster?"

Blossom hesitated. "Is that what they're wearing to parties these days?"

"Absolutely," Pete said. He was wearing a white linen jacket over a navy blue T-shirt.

"You look a lot prettier than I do," I said glumly.

"You look lovely, Holly," Birdie said. "Blossom's just an old-fashioned fuddy-duddy. She doesn't know what young people wear anymore."

"That's true," Blossom agreed.

On a scale of one to ten, my self-confidence was a three. Pete told Blossom where we'd be in case she needed me.

I almost wished she needed me now.

*   *   *

An hour later I was glad that I'd gone. The party was outdoors, at someone's pool, and since people kept jumping into the water and being pushed in, it hardly mattered what anyone was wearing.

Colored lights and paper lanterns were strung from awnings and tree branches. The music was loud, there were tables set out with food, and the whole atmosphere was cheery and festive. I'd almost forgotten what parties were like. I couldn't remember the last time I'd been to one.

Pete introduced me to the hostess, Diane Seville, obviously a rich summer person, but democratic. There was a good mix of summer people and islanders, and Diane didn't think, as Chandra did, that working for a living was a disgrace.

Pete hadn't told her that I worked for the Brewsters, just that I was staying with them. I thought that was very tactful. Even if she knew I was a companion, I didn't think Diane would turn away in disgust. She was friendly and gracious, and she helped me push Pete into the pool.

By that time the party was very lively. The music grew louder, and I was talking and joking with people I'd never met before as if we'd been partying for years.

Later on, after I'd met almost everyone at the party, Diane and a boy named Mike sneaked up behind me and threw me into the pool.

It was a wonderful moment. I came up choking and sputtering, but I felt great. They had welcomed me. After all, you don't throw a stranger into your swimming pool.

I shook my fist at them and swam for the ladder at

the deep end of the pool. "I'll get you!" I warned. I hoisted myself out of the water, and there, sitting on the diving board with her hands clasped around her knees, was Chandra.

My first impulse was to throw myself back into the pool and not come up till Labor Day. It was an impulse I should have followed.

I quickly walked away from her, around the edge of the pool, and pretended to be concerned about my wet hair and clothes.

I met Pete at the punch bowl. He ladled me out a cup of punch that I drank without tasting. He couldn't have seen Chandra yet, or he would have warned me.

Diane and Mike approached us, snickering like naughty children. "I'm sorry, Holly," Diane said. "I hope you won't hold this against me."

"No, that's okay. But I really should go home and change into dry clothes." And not come back till Labor Day.

"Why?" asked Mike. "Everybody's wet."

Diane nodded. "See Pete?" she said. "He looks like a drowned rat."

"Thank you," Pete said.

Through all of this banter, I was the only one who saw that Chandra was headed toward us, and that there was no way to escape her before the explosion.

"What's *she* doing here?" Chandra demanded.

"*She's* leaving," I said. I turned away, but Pete took my arm.

"This is Holly Campion," Diane said. "She came with Pete."

"I know who she is," Chandra said. "I want to know why you let her come."

"What's the matter with you?" Diane asked. "Why shouldn't Holly come?"

I wished she hadn't asked that.

"She doesn't belong here. And she knew Pete was going with me."

"Wait a minute," Pete said loudly.

I tried to pull away, but he wouldn't let go of my arm. The sounds of the party faded away. No splashing, no laughing—some thoughtful person had even turned down the stereo.

"I have to get out of here," I urged Pete. *"Let go of me."*

"Chandra, stop it," Diane said angrily. "This is my party and Holly's my guest."

"And you're my cousin!" Chandra shouted.

"Cousin?" I finally wrenched my arm away from Pete's grasp. "How could you do this to me? Why didn't you tell me she—"

Pete wouldn't look me in the eye. "I thought—"

"Listen, Chandra." I was seething. "I am not interested in Pete. He's just a friend. He *used* to be a friend."

Pete turned away. He was the only guest at the party not staring at me.

"So do me a favor." My voice shook and I felt chilled in my wet clothes. "You can have Pete, but don't you ever come near me again."

I brushed my way past clusters of people who parted like the Red Sea to let me through. I had to get out of there. In fact, I probably had to get off Harmony Island.

I could never face those people again. At least when she'd screamed at me in town I didn't know any of the passersby. It's a lot more humiliating to be attacked in front of people you know.

I could imagine them gossiping about me for the rest of the summer, telling anyone who didn't already know about me all the details of our stupid little triangle.

"Holly, wait! Wait a minute!" Diane ran after me. "Holly, I'm really sorry."

"It's not your fault."

"Holly, she's a creep. She may be my cousin, but she *is* a creep. Everybody thinks so."

Then why, I wanted to ask, do you invite her to your parties? But I knew the answer. Chandra might be a creep, but she was family.

I shook my head. "It's okay. I'm getting cold. I was ready to go home anyway."

I saw Pete coming toward us, and I turned away from him. I started down the long driveway toward the road.

He caught up with me and planted himself in my path. "I'll take you home," he said.

"I'd rather walk," I said.

"It's too far and it's too dark. Listen, I'm sorry. I should have told you they were cousins. I don't want you to be mad at me."

"Too bad."

"Did you really mean what you said? About not being interested in me?"

"Yes." I stepped around him and started to walk away.

"Why didn't you tell me? You knew how much I liked you."

Good question. I didn't have an answer.

"I just wanted to be friends," I said.

"Friends don't kiss like that!"

I started walking again.

"I don't believe this," he said. "You never liked me?"

"I liked you. I just don't have romantic feelings for you. Leave me alone. I want to go home."

"I'll drive you." He sounded like he was trying to talk from between clenched teeth. "It's too dangerous to walk." He took my arm firmly and led me to the truck. I let him. I could never have found my way to the Brewsters' house.

We rode in silence. Pete drew up in front of the garage.

"Just tell me one thing," he said. "Is there someone else?"

"Yes," I admitted.

"Was there someone else all along?"

"I should have told you."

"Yeah, it would have been easier that way," he said.

Angry as I was, I knew I was wrong about this. I had managed to kid myself for a while, thinking that there was no reason to tell Pete about Avery. But I was wrong. I'd been wrong from the beginning. Friends *don't* kiss like that.

I let myself out of the truck and walked up the front steps. I opened the door without looking back. I heard the truck take off, the tires chewing up the grass as he peeled out.

Birdie was standing in the hall as I let myself in. Her eyes were bright and she smiled impishly. "Did you have a good time?"

"No," I said. "I didn't."

14

I had to shop in town three times that week, and sure enough, I ran into several people I'd met at the party. They all stopped to say hello, but I knew what they were thinking. I mumbled a greeting at anyone who spoke to me, but I hurried away as fast as I could.

It was awful. If I hadn't had Avery's visit to look forward to I don't know how I would have forced myself to stay there.

This time Avery phoned Wednesday to assure us that he was coming.

"And he said he has a surprise for us," Blossom said. "I wonder what it is."

"Maybe he's married!" Birdie said excitedly.

"Don't be silly," Blossom said. "He hasn't even got a girlfriend. It's probably a present."

I welcomed all the work Blossom found for me to

do on Sunday and Monday. I did the laundry, dusted, prepared breakfast and lunch—I even ironed a tablecloth. I straightened the kitchen cabinets, which hardly needed straightening, and alphabetized the pill bottles in the medicine cabinet, which drove Birdie nuts when she tried to find her phenolphthalein.

With Blossom's help, I kept myself busy, and by keeping myself busy, I had less time to brood.

Tuesday was my day off, and since there was no one on the island that I wanted to spend it with, I called my mother. If my father was feeling better I would visit them. And if not, maybe she and I could meet for lunch.

I wanted to be someone's daughter again.

But no one answered the phone. And no one answered the phone when I tried again a half hour later.

"Why don't you go to the beach?" Birdie suggested.

I couldn't explain that there were too many people at the beach that I didn't want to see.

"I'll try them again later." But I spent the rest of the day reading Agatha Christie and watching soap operas I hadn't followed for years.

We ate lunch while we watched *Divorce Court*, to which I was becoming morbidly addicted.

On Wednesday and Thursday I actually asked Blossom for more work. I was certain I was having a mental breakdown.

"Do you know how to fix the butterfly *valvo*?" she asked.

"Yes, I told you I did. Why don't you come out and watch me?"

"*Bono ideo!*"

We went out to the garage, and I demonstrated, with very little hesitation, my knowledge of butterfly *valvo* fixing.

"Ta da!" I started the car.

"Bonega!"

"Your bone aches?" I guessed.

"An excellent job," Blossom corrected. "But I must say you're not doing very well with your Esperanto."

I did the shopping for the weekend on Thursday. I stopped at the bookstore and picked up two more Agatha Christies, along with some books Blossom had ordered.

I bought candles at Wickworld and groceries at the Superette, and I was recognized by a lot of people I didn't want to see.

I bought a box of chocolate-chip cookie mix. We had made Christmas cookies at home for years. Maybe I wasn't up to pie baking, but I was sure I could handle cookies, and I wanted to do something special for Avery.

Blossom scowled at the package. "Cookies from a mix? I always make cookies from scratch."

"You know how to bake and I don't," I said. "Remember my pie crust."

She shuddered. "I'm sure Avery will appreciate the cookies. Even if they are from a mix."

The cookies were much easier to make than the pie. They didn't have to be rolled out, just dropped from a spoon onto the baking sheets.

By eleven o'clock Friday morning my spirits had lifted. The house smelled of chocolate and brown sugar, and it was impossible, I decided, to remain depressed while chocolate-chip cookies were baking.

Besides, by then I only had to wait three more hours for Avery, who was taking the one-fifteen ferry. That gave me time to wash my hair and pick out something to wear from my wardrobe of absolutely nothing more glamorous than a T-shirt with red glitter on the front.

I would definitely have to do some shopping. What if Avery wanted to take me someplace? What if he invited me to dinner at a fancy restaurant? And even if he didn't, all the clothes I had made me look too young.

I hadn't seen or spoken to Pete since the party. When I got to the ferry dock I parked as far as I could from the boat shop and waited in the hearse until the passengers began to disembark.

I got out of the car and walked toward the dock, trying to pick Avery out of the crowd. Finally I spotted him.

"Avery!" I yelled. "Here I am!" I sounded much too eager and excited, but I couldn't help it.

He saw me and waved, and then he put his arm around a woman walking beside him. A tall, silver-blond, leggy woman, wearing white shorts and a tropical blouse. Thin thighs.

No. No, no, no. The woman is a cousin. But Avery said that his aunts were all the family he had.

She is his assistant from work. He's giving her a special treat for the weekend. He probably does this once or twice a season—gives the little people a taste of the good life.

No. If he wanted to give her a treat he would have taken her to Bermuda, not to visit his aunts.

I think my mouth was still open and I was silently repeating "no, no" when they reached me.

"You certainly look surprised," Avery said.

I looked like a blowfish, and my eyes must have been popping out of my face.

"This is my fiancée, Lorelei Hudnut. Holly is the girl who's staying with my aunts."

Fiancée. Bride to be. Love of his life. Mother of his children.

Noooo!

I drove back to the house with reckless disregard for life and limb. I zipped along at thirty-five miles an hour, not caring whether we hit anything or not.

"I see you've gotten used to the car," Avery said.

I cursed the car under my breath.

"What a lovely place," Lorelei said.

Drop dead, Blondie.

Birdie and Blossom went bonkers.

"I knew it, I knew it," Birdie said. "I told you, didn't I, Blossom?"

"You said they were married," Blossom reminded her. "But this is almost as good." She was beaming.

"Soon we'll be great aunts!" Birdie couldn't contain her excitement. "Look at the two of them. Won't their children be beautiful!"

I nearly threw up.

"You told me your aunts were nice," Lorelei cooed, "but you didn't tell me they were *this* nice."

Give me a break.

Later Avery handed me an envelope. "There's two weeks' salary."

What made him think I was going to stay any more weeks? As far as I was concerned, my sojourn on Harmony Island was history.

I'd stay for this weekend, in the event that Lorelei might drown, but if she didn't, I was out of here.

How much can a person stand? I couldn't look anyone in town in the eye because of what happened at Diane's party, Pete would probably never talk to me again—and who could blame him?—and now this.

No. Not even for eight dollars an hour.

Avery wanted to take Lorelei to the beach. "Why don't we all go together?" Lorelei said.

The aunts had their bathing suits on practically before she finished her sentence.

"Don't you want to come, Holly?" he asked, when I made no move toward beachwear. "It's a beautiful day."

It's a scummy day. It's a scummy day following a rotten week, preceded by a disgusting weekend.

I tried to maintain my dignity. "I think not."

I knew that I needed time alone to throw myself onto my bed and into a tantrum.

Blossom made a big deal out of my homemade cookies, which was hardly in character. Avery and Lorelei also made a big deal out of them.

"You baked these *yourself?*" Lorelei pretended to be impressed.

"I added water."

"My goodness," Lorelei said, "I wouldn't even know how to do that."

I didn't doubt it for a minute.

"But you won't have to, honey," Avery said.

I'll kill her. I'll kill him.

"What do you do, dear?" Birdie asked.

"Do?" She looked puzzled. "Well . . . I like to shop."

"She means what kind of a job do you have?" Blossom explained.

"Job? Well, I don't actually have a job."

"She doesn't need a job," Avery said, looking smug. "She's got me."

I wish I had eaten all the cookies myself.

The woman was a slug, a leech. A parasite sucking at Avery's money. She *shopped*. What kind of a life was that?

A pretty pleasant life, I recalled. The kind of life I'd had for seventeen years, and the kind of life I'd hoped to return to with Avery.

But I was different from Lorelei. At least I was different enough to recognize how alike we were.

With Birdie's help I cleared away the dinner dishes. I heard Blossom talking about candles.

A ray of hope. Lorelei might think twice about marrying a man with a crazy aunt.

"How exciting!" She had a shrill, little-girl voice. "I've never been to a seance."

Blossom popped into the kitchen. "Come on, Holly, we're starting."

"I have a really bad headache." It was a lie, but the way things were going I was sure to have one any minute now.

"Would you like some camomile tea?" Blossom asked. "It's very good for headaches."

"No. I'll just finish the dishes and go to bed."

"Don't worry about the dishes. Just go to bed," Blossom advised.

The four of them wished me a speedy recovery.

But I knew that the only way I'd recover from what I had was if Avery suddenly realized that Lorelei was nothing but a passing fancy, and *I* was his real key to happiness.

Chances were this was going to be a long illness.

15

I don't know how I got through the rest of that weekend. Yes, I do know. I wallowed in self-pity and dreamed up a number of hideous things that I hoped would happen to Lorelei.

It seemed that Edmund was very pleased with Avery's choice of a mate. Birdie told me that he had said this was the major change he'd predicted.

"There was no danger after all," Birdie told me. "Blossom must have misunderstood."

Sunday morning Avery went boating with Lorelei. To Pirates' Cove. His private island. With no one around to interfere with their heavy-duty smooching session. How disgusting.

It was my day off, and there was no place on the island I wanted to be. I called home.

My mother sounded delighted to hear from me.

"When are you coming home?" she asked.

"To stay?"

"To visit. We haven't seen you in three weeks."

"I know. How about today?"

"Wonderful! Your father will be so pleased."

"Will he really?" My father hadn't been pleased with anything for two months.

"He's much better, Holly. He misses you a lot. We'll talk when you get here. I'll meet you at the ferry. What time?"

I looked at my watch. "There's a ferry in an hour. I can be there by twelve-thirty."

Blossom drove me down to the dock. She and Birdie waved as I stood at the rail, the ferry chugging away from the pier.

I waved back, seeing them and the island grow smaller and smaller, until, if I turned my head toward the bay I could forget that I'd ever been there.

My mother looked great. And my father was a changed man. The house would have to be sold, and my mother would have to work, but they had plans. They sounded almost excited about starting a new life. My father's pessimism had been replaced by ideas and anticipation.

"I've been thinking," he said, as we sat down to a late brunch at the Bayberrry House. "Couldn't you go to Unity and live at home? You could work part-time."

"But, Dad, I don't want to go to Unity. I'd rather save my money till I can afford Sarah Lawrence."

"Then why don't you find a job where you can stay with us?"

"I was thinking about that," I said.

He smiled delightedly.

"Don't you like the job you have?" my mother asked.

"It's kind of isolated. I think it will be pretty bleak in the winter."

"Holly! I can't believe it! Is it really you?"

I turned, and my old friend, Jane Schuster, bent down and threw her arms around my neck.

"Jane!" I jumped up and we bumped foreheads. "It's so good to see you."

In an instant I saw what I had left behind—good friends, love, memories, possibilities. Long before I went to Harmony Island I had marooned myself on an island of my own.

I hugged Jane so hard she squealed. "I see you've got your strength back," she joked. "Are you home to stay?"

"Not this time. But I think I will be soon. It's just—well, we're going to sell the house . . ." I didn't want to say any more in front of my parents, but I was eager to tell Jane everything. Everything I'd wanted to hide since April. I couldn't remember why I wanted to keep this a secret. What had I been so ashamed of?

"We have to live somewhere," my father said. "Maybe we can find an apartment around here."

The four of us had lived in a ten-room house. How were we going to fit our lives into an apartment?

My father looked at me hopefully, like he wanted my approval.

We would manage. Other people did.

"It would be great," I said, "if we could stay somewhere around here."

"It would," Jane agreed. "You know, everyone's been asking about you. I have a million things to tell you."

"Why don't we get a table together?" my mother suggested. "Are your parents with you, Jane?"

"We were supposed to meet—there they are."

The Schusters smiled broadly when they saw us.

"Holly! What a surprise!" Mrs. Schuster said. "And we haven't seen you two in ages," she said to my parents. They arranged to sit together. "Why don't you girls take another table?" my mother suggested. "We'll have Holly all afternoon."

I ate bacon, sausage, and ham with my pancakes, to make up for the meatless weeks at Blossom's house. I drank seven cups of tea. We didn't stop talking for two hours.

It was glorious.

I hated to go back to the island, but I couldn't just walk away from Blossom and Birdie without advance warning. I knew they depended on me, even though Blossom didn't like to admit it.

Her hip was getting worse. She used the cane all the time now, and I was sure her limp was more pronounced than ever, but she wouldn't admit that either.

I called to find out when Avery and his bimbo were leaving, so I wouldn't have to see them again.

"Why don't you stay over?" Birdie said. "A girl should spend time with her family."

It was so tempting.

It was too tempting. If I stayed here overnight, I would never go back to the Brewsters. I wouldn't have had the strength of character to force myself back on that ferry, back into that house, after spending today with people who loved me.

This was my reality. My parents, Jane, my friends. *This* was where my life was. Harmony Island was just a mirage.

"No, I'll come back tonight," I said. Just for a little while. Just temporarily. Until they find someone else, or Blossom gets better. In a few days, I'd be back where I belonged.

I had forgotten how musty and dank the house smelled. I must have gotten used to it while I was living there.

And in my green-and-yellow-and-orange room, it seemed that home was the mirage—a fantasy so brief it might never have happened.

"Mrs. Brewster's hip seems to be getting worse," I told Birdie the next day.

We were about to start on her memoirs, but she closed the scrapbook she'd been skimming and gave me a troubled look. "I know it. I've tried to get her to see the surgeon, but she won't even talk to me about it. But you can tell that every step she takes is a struggle."

"Can't anything be done?" I asked.

"I don't know," Birdie said. "If she won't see the doctor we'll never know. I'm so glad you're here, Holly."

Please don't say that. Not when I have to tell you I'm quitting.

"Maybe you can convince her," Birdie said. "Maybe she'll listen to you."

"Why should she listen to me?"

"She thinks a great deal of you," Birdie replied.

"I didn't know that." Although Blossom had definitely softened in the past week, I didn't think she would give much weight to my advice.

"And you're an objective judge," she added. "Avery and I are relatives. She thinks we worry too much. But if she sees that you're concerned too . . ."

"I'll try," I said. It was the least I could do before I told them I was leaving.

Blossom looked up from her copy of *Fate*. "Haven't you started the *tolajo* yet? They're forecasting rain for the *posttagmezo*."

"The postage meter?" I asked.

"Afternoon. You don't seem to be very apt at languages."

Anticipating washing and hanging the *talajo* strengthened my resolve to quit. But first: "Birdie is worried about you."

"Birdie's always worried about something," Blossom said.

"Well, maybe. But I'm worried too. I think your limp has gotten worse since I've been here. Don't you think you should see a doctor?"

"What do you suppose the doctor would tell me?" She slapped the magazine down on the coffee table. "What do you think the doctor can do? I broke my hip. They put a pin in it. There's nothing else they can do."

"How do you know that if you don't ask?" I persisted.

"And have another operation? How do you think I got like this? I will never see another surgeon again as long as I live."

"But maybe a physical therapist? I understand how you feel, but—"

"No, you don't," she snapped. "You couldn't possibly know how I feel."

"All right, that's true. But at least a prescription for painkillers when its gets bad?"

"I don't take drugs," she said. "Now don't you think you'd better get to the laundry?"

I thought about my hours at home as I did the laundry, remembering them and contemplating a happy—if impoverished—future.

I'd liked being rich. You'd have to be an idiot not to prefer it to being poor, but I'd taken the first steps to reclaiming the really important things in my life.

Home had nothing to do with money.

Between washloads Birdie tried to dictate some of her memoirs, but it was hard for her to concentrate after she heard Blossom's response to our talk.

And it was hard for me to concentrate while I tried to tell them I wanted to quit.

The sooner I told them, the sooner they could start looking for my replacement, and the sooner I'd get on with the rest of my life.

But how easy would it be to replace me? I only got the job because no one else wanted it. Finding a new companion could take weeks, and I wanted to go home *now*.

I prepared lunch and watched *Divorce Court* with them. This would be my legacy from Harmony Island—an addiction to *Divorce Court*.

Really, all that was required of me was to give them

two weeks notice. That was standard business practice. It wasn't my responsibility to stay until they hired someone else.

Besides, Avery's tootsie was going to be their niece-in-law. Let her worry about them.

I'll tell them after I wash the lunch dishes, I thought. But after I put away the lunch dishes I decided to tell them at dinner.

But at dinner I figured I ought to wait till they finished eating, so as not to bring up an unpleasant subject while they were digesting.

Why did I feel so guilty about leaving this place? It was impossible for me to stay. I had lost my only friend, I didn't have the nerve to try to make others, and if I had to endure another weekend with Lorelei I would slip rat poison into her wheat germ.

Yet we finished dinner, I did the dishes, and I still couldn't tell them.

They needed me. Even though Blossom tried to hide her growing dependency, they needed me. That was the problem. I'd never had to take care of anyone but myself, and with money and maids, that was a pretty cushy job.

I wasn't used to being needed.

But I had to be responsible for my own life now. No one was going to take care of me but me.

Tomorrow, I promised myself as I got into bed, I'll tell them tomorrow for sure.

16

I woke in the middle of a raging thunderstorm. I looked at my clock as a blaze of lightning lit up the room. It was two-twenty.

Lightning bolts were coming one after another, so rapidly that it seemed like the storm was centered right over our house.

I'd never heard thunder so loud—ear-splitting claps that made me want to dive under the covers so I wouldn't have to see or hear the storm's violence. A perfect night to shoot the vampire worm movie.

The next bolt of lightning looked like it struck barely two feet from my window. I shrieked, and burrowed under the blanket. I pulled in my pillow after me. I intended to stay there until the storm was over.

Not a very mature approach to a dangerous weather phenomenon, but no one could see me, and I didn't know what else I could do to calm down.

I thought I heard a faint voice in between thunderbolts, and while it was probably the rain or the wind, I peeked out from under the covers.

The door to my room flew open. Lightning framed Birdie in the doorway, her feet bare, her hair in curlers, her red robe clutched at the waist.

"Holly, it's Blossom. Come on."

"What's wrong?" I jumped out of bed and tried to switch on the lamp next to my bed. Nothing happened.

"The electricity's out," Birdie said. "Come *on*."

Blossom was crouched down in front of the bathroom door. I could only see her in segments, as lightning flashed. She was doubled over in pain. Her fist was pressed against her chest, and I could hear her struggling for breath.

"Get a flashlight, Birdie. And a blanket."

"Doctor," Blossom gasped. "Call the doctor."

"Oh, my God," Birdie wailed. "She *must* be sick."

Birdie groped to the linen closet and came back with a flashlight. I took it and shone it on Blossom's face. Beads of perspiration dotted her forehead and upper lip, and her skin looked dull and pasty.

I handed Birdie back the flashlight. "Call the fire department. Tell them it's an emergency."

Did I sound calm? I felt absolute terror kneeling over Blossom. I was sure she was having a heart attack, and while I had never seen a heart attack victim, Blossom looked only a few breaths short of dying.

I covered her with a blanket and patted her shoulder.

"Hold on, Mrs. Brewster. Birdie's going to call the ambulance."

Then Birdie's scream from downstairs: "I can't get a dial tone! I can't get *anything*."

"Dying," Blossom whispered. "Heart. Going to die."

"The hell you are!" I shouted. Even though I thought she was right. "Come on, Birdie. We'll take her to the firehouse ourselves."

"How?" Birdie hurried back upstairs.

How? I had no idea how. Could we carry her down the stairs and out to the garage? If she tried to walk, would that be the final strain that would kill her?

"Get her shoes and raincoat," I said, trying to think. "And get my shoes. I'll bring the car right up to the back door."

Now all we had to do was get her down the stairs. "Danger." Birdie dropped my shoes. "Edmund meant danger all along." She pushed Blossom's slippers onto her feet.

I stepped into my sneakers.

"We have to get you downstairs, Mrs. Brewster. To the car. Everything's going to be okay."

The only thing I could think of was to have her lean most of her weight on me while Birdie held onto one of her arms, sort of pulling Blossom down the steps without making her do real walking.

"You're going to have to help, Mrs. Brewster." I hauled her arm around my neck, and Birdie tried to take her other arm. But the stairs were too narrow for us to walk down three abreast.

I couldn't pretend to be calm anymore. I felt a spiraling sense of panic that made my own heart threaten to stop and that blocked rational thought from my mind.

Stupid, I thought. Stupid. The most important thing in dealing with a heart attack is time, and we're wasting it.

"What are we going to do?" Birdie asked. "We'll never get down this way."

Finally my brain started to work again. "I'll go. You stay here with Blossom and I'll go to the firehouse and bring them. Hang on, Mrs. Brewster," I pleaded.

I had to take the flashlight with me to get to the garage, but I would bring it back once I had the car's headlights on.

I was soaked just running to the garage. I unlocked the doors and pulled them open. I jumped into the hearse and the engine made that horrible wheezing sound, and died.

"Not now!" I screamed. I tried it again. Again, wheeze, choke, nothing.

I jumped out of the car and yanked up the hood. I held the flashlight with one hand and began to fumble with the nut on top of the oil filter. I needed two more hands . . . to pray with. I wasn't sure I remembered the drill.

I got the filter off and held the flashlight so that I could see the valve. I had to wedge it open with something, so I ran outside and scrambled around on the ground till I found a small stick. I pushed the valve open with the stick.

I got back into the car and turned the ignition key. The engine roared to life. I wanted to cheer, but I couldn't spare the time. Everything was taking so *long*. I couldn't begin to imagine how much time I'd already wasted and how time was still running away from me.

I removed the stick and replaced the top of the oil filter.

The wind blew me back to the house. I yelled to

Birdie that I was leaving the flashlight, and I grabbed a red slicker from a hook at the kitchen door.

I ran back to the car, but I ran as if in a bad dream, where you go as fast as you can but your legs are made of marshmallows.

The rain was still heavy as I pulled out of the garage. There were a few flashes of lightning, but they weren't nearby anymore.

I was so scared about Blossom that I forgot that I was afraid to drive the hearse. I drove as if I were in Chandra's Jaguar, with absolutely no regard for speed limits, safety precautions, or oncoming cars.

Of which, thank God, there weren't any.

I leaned on the horn the moment I hit Main Street. I screeched around a corner, still honking, and skidded to a stop across the street from the firehouse.

There was a light shining in the back, behind a shiny red emergency truck.

"The Brewsters!" I yelled. "Heart attack. Hurry!"

Three men came running. Two of them jumped into the emergency truck and took off, siren screaming. One stayed behind to sound the alarm signal. Then he ran toward a second truck. I was so rattled that it hardly even registered that the third man was Pete.

"Get in," he ordered. *"Move!"*

I pulled myself into the truck. I was slammed back against the seat as we zoomed out of the firehouse.

"The phone doesn't work," I explained. "Blossom's having a heart attack. We couldn't get her down the stairs. Couldn't call the doctor—"

I was sure that she was dead by now.

"I took too long." I was ready to burst into tears.

"I just couldn't think straight. And that stupid hearse wouldn't start—"

Now I was crying, frustrated by my own stupidity. Blossom was dead, and it was my fault for taking so long to get help.

Pete drove like a demon, paying no attention to my tears or to the storm. The first truck reached the house before us. Its blue light flashed, and the siren still screamed even though the truck had stopped.

Pete jumped out of the truck and ran into the house.

Another car followed us onto the grass, stopping just next to the first emergency truck. A woman in a plastic rain hat stuck her head out of the window. "Where?"

"This way," I said, "upstairs." I ran into the kitchen with her right behind me. She was carrying a blue case with a cross on it. She brushed past me heading for the stairs.

Two men were just bringing Blossom down, carefully, deliberately, on a stretcher. Pete walked backward ahead of them carrying a large lantern. I didn't know if Blossom was alive or dead.

"Get out of the way," Pete said. I couldn't see very well as they carried her past me. I got a glimpse of her face in the lantern light. Her eyes were half-closed and her mouth was open slackly.

They carried her outside.

"I want to go with her!" Birdie cried. She ran after them, splashing through the mud, her feet still bare.

"There's no room." The woman who had arrived last climbed into the ambulance ahead of the stretcher.

"She's my sister!" Birdie shrieked. "I have to go with her!"

"You come with me, Birdie," Pete said. "We'll follow right behind them."

"Oh, yes!" She slogged to the truck.

"Where are you taking Blossom?" I called.

"Emergency clinic."

"I didn't know there was an emergency clinic," I said pointlessly. "I didn't know you were a fireman."

But he was gone. They were all gone. There was nothing I could do but wait.

17

They let me visit Blossom in the intensive care unit the next day, but only because Birdie said I was a member of the family. Even then I was only allowed five minutes.

I wanted to see for myself that she was all right, that she was still alive. Until I did, I couldn't erase the memory of my last glimpse of her on the stretcher.

She had IV lines in her arms, thin plastic tubes in her nostrils, and wires that hooked her up to a computer screen.

Her eyes were closed.

"Mrs. Brewster?" I whispered.

Her eyes opened. She smiled with genuine affection when she saw me.

"How are you feeling?" Stupid question. She'd had a heart attack. How should she be feeling? But what was more important than that?

"*Malgrandpeca,*" she murmured.

"Like a giant woodpecker?" I guessed.

"I feel fine," she corrected me. "Thank you for saving my life."

"I didn't really save your life," I said. "Birdie told me it was just a minor angina attack."

"Don't argue with me," she said. "I'm the patient and it was my angina attack."

"Well, I'm just glad you're alive."

"Ditto," she said. "Is Avery here?"

"Not yet. He was in Baltimore. He's taking the first plane he can get."

"Time's up!" A nurse bustled in and started shooing me toward the door. It was just as well, because Blossom seemed too weak to talk much more. Even though her skin color was back to normal, attached to tubes and bags and monitors and needles, she looked so helpless.

I could never have imagined Blossom being helpless.

"Good-bye, Mrs. Brewster," I said. "I'll see you later."

She nodded slightly. "Call me Blossom," she whispered.

Pete was sitting on a turquoise plastic chair in the clinic's waiting room when the nurse ushered me out. He carried a bunch of carnations.

"No flowers," the nurse said sternly.

"I told Birdie to get something to eat at the Chat 'n' Nibble," he said. "Are you going to stay here?"

"Of course I will," I said. "Where else would I be?"

He handed me the bouquet. "Then hold these till I come back."

Why had I said that, where else would I be? Why

should I be here at all? I could go back to the house and have Birdie call me when she wanted to be picked up from the clinic. I didn't have to stay and hold her hand all day.

And why worry about Blossom? The doctors said she was going to be fine in a few weeks. Birdie even persuaded her to let the doctor schedule X rays of her hip before she was discharged.

There was absolutely no reason for me to linger on Harmony Island. All right, I might have to stay a little longer than I'd expected, but only to get Blossom through the convalescence period. A couple of weeks, tops.

Meanwhile they could advertise for a new companion.

They didn't need me. Anyone who could dial a phone and drive a hearse would do.

Pete was back in less than five minutes.

"You're not a member of the family," I said. "How come they let you visit?"

"They know me."

Even though I would leave soon I couldn't go without apologizing to Pete.

"You were terrific last night," I began. "What would we have done without you?"

"There would have been another volunteer. There are three on all the time."

He seemed so indifferent that it was hard for me to pull words out. "I'm sorry."

"About what?" he asked.

"The party. Everything I said."

He shrugged. "It doesn't seem to matter much now, does it?"

"Nothing seems to matter much now," I said. After all, compared to life and death, was Chandra Gaines worth hating? Was an outburst at a party any reason to give up seeing people again?

Did it make any difference that Blossom didn't have an electric can opener? Did it matter that I wasn't rich?

I was young. I was alive. There were people who loved me.

"I wouldn't want anything to happen without my telling you how much your friendship meant." It was hard to say, but I was glad I said it.

"I'm sorry too," he said. "I should have warned you about Chandra. But it didn't do my ego any good when you handed me to her."

"I didn't really mean it," I said. "I was just angry. You're much too good for her."

Just then Avery came sprinting down the corridor carrying a leather briefcase. "Is Blossom all right?" he called. "How is she?"

"She's going to be fine," I said. "She's waiting to see you." I pointed to the ICU. He hurried off.

Even my love for Avery seemed pale and insignificant now. He loved someone else. Okay. So did I.

I was astonished to think it. I really did care about Blossom and Birdie. Blossom wasn't as easy to love as Birdie, but she needed me, and she wanted me to call her Blossom.

How could I leave them now? I wanted to stay long enough to see Blossom free of tubes and IV bags. I wanted to see her swim in the bay, graceful as a dolphin.

I wanted to see Birdie smile. A real smile, not a

brave little pretense of a smile that she put on in the clinic. I wanted to hear her giggle about her honeymoon, and argue with Blossom about pistachio ice cream.

I didn't want to leave. Not yet. I wanted to take care of Blossom and Birdie. Maybe I was crazy, but it felt good to be needed.

I could stay for six months. Long enough to make sure that Blossom was well, and long enough to find someone else who would care about them. Just long enough to reassure myself that they would be okay.

I could start Sarah Lawrence in January. I'd have enough money saved up by then for the spring semester, and that's as far ahead as I wanted to think.

"Holly?" Pete sat down next to me on a plastic chair. "I know there's someone else, but we can still be friends, can't we?"

I looked down the hall to see Birdie trudging toward us. She waved at me, and her face brightened.

"There's no one else," I said. "At least, not the way you mean. And we can still be friends."

"Oh, Holly." Birdie sighed heavily and sank down on a plastic chair next to me. She took my hand, clasping it as hard as she was able. "I'm awfully glad you're here."

I squeezed her hand gently. "So am I."

ABOUT THE AUTHOR

ELLEN CONFORD is the author of more than thirty books for children and young adults. She is a native New Yorker who now lives in Great Neck, New York, with her husband, David. She is a championship-level Scrabble player, and also competes in crossword-puzzle tournaments. Her other popular novels available in Bantam Starfire paperback editions are *Hail, Hail Camp Timberwood, Anything for a Friend, The Things I Did for Love,* and *Genie With the Light Blue Hair.*